Ode Kimball

D0407370

My 13th Season

My 13th Season

Kristi Roberts

Henry Holt and Company

New York

Henry Holt and Company, LLC
Publishers since 1866
115 West 18th Street
New York, New York 10011
www.henryholt.com

Henry Holt is a registered trademark of Henry Holt and Company, LLC
Distributed in Canada by H. B. Fenn and Company Ltd.

Library of Congress Cataloging-in-Publication Data
Roberts, Kristi.
My thirteenth season / Kristi Roberts.—1st ed.
p.   cm.
Summary: Already downhearted due to the loss of her mother and her father's
overwhelming grief, thirteen-year-old Fran decides to give up her dream of becoming
the first female in professional baseball after a coach attacks her just for being a girl.
ISBN-13: 978-0-8050-7495-6
ISBN-10: 0-8050-7495-3
1. Baseball—Fiction.   2. Sex role—Fiction.   3. Fathers and daughters—Fiction.
4. Grief—Fiction.   5. Teamwork (Sports)—Fiction.   6. Oregon—Fiction.
I. Title.
PZ7.R54327My 2005   [Fic]—dc22   2004052368
First Edition—2005
Printed in the United States of America on acid-free paper. ∞

10   9   8   7   6   5   4   3   2   1

For Mom and Dad,
who always cheered me on

c h a p t e r 1

"Girl germs," Billy Smythe sneered. It was a kinder-
garten taunt, just plain dumb, but his buddies still
snickered as Billy pulled a bandana out of his back
pocket and made a big show of wiping down the bat I
had just dropped.

I pulled my cap lower over my forehead and gave
Billy my best Evil Eye. He gave me one back.

"Don't count on a career in comedy, Smythe," I said.

Billy sneered at me again. Touching his right nostril with his upper lip was his favorite thing to do
with his face. But I'd rattled him. Our pitcher tossed
a ball so easy it might as well have been underhand.
Billy swung. Missed.

"Good! Swing! Billy!" puffed MacKenzie Wheeler, Tiffany Daniels, and Selena Jones, the Three Most Popular Girls in Junior High, as they swung their legs in a complicated cheerleading kick.

"Nice form, kid," said Coach Foster.

"Did you consider hitting the ball?" I asked.

The coach glowered at me. Billy shot me a look full of razors and knives, and the rest of the team discussed assassination.

I'd been putting up with this abuse for a solid month now. My father and I had moved over to South Highwater last fall, but I'd missed Junior League registration (this town was a little old-fashioned—the information didn't go out to girls). By the time I signed up, the only spot left was on the Highwater Hardwares. At school I heard rumors. The coach was a badass. Kids would play for a few weeks and then quit. The ones who stayed were there because their truant officers made them.

So I figured they'd be thrilled to have me. I had two Golden Gloves and a spot on last year's Willamette League All Stars team to prove my ability. But the coach took one look at my blond hair and my braids and screamed, "Over my dead body!" It took a personal visit from the county sheriff to convince Coach Ronald Foster that there was a girl on his team.

Nothing could be as hard as what I'd gone through lately, though, so I was optimistic. Sure, I trash-talked Billy, but I was going to prove myself to these guys. For three straight weeks I'd been playing my all-time personal best. Two days ago I had three hits and five RBIs. Still . . . no high-fives, not one slap on the back, not even a faint "whoopee" from the dugout. They only had eight players; still they didn't want me.

One thing kept me psyched: Steven Chauppette, my best friend from third grade, was on the team. He'd moved to L.A. two years ago, then this spring, after his parents' divorce, he and his mother had moved back and settled in South Highwater. With all that unpacking, Steven had missed registration and got stuck on the Hardwares, too. Every time I got discouraged, he was there with a thumbs-up and a smile. He'd walk me home and we'd swap memories about our old team, the Rosewood Grocery Baggers. He said not to worry, the Hardwares were good guys, really, and if I kept on playing so well they'd have to accept me.

But that didn't happen. Today was proof.

"Coach, I have some team business." A big kid called Mozzie Meeker struggled across the field toward our pre-game warm-up, waving his hand in the air. Little Blast Neukum hustled along beside him.

Hootie held his pitch and Billy settled the bat on

his shoulder. Coach Foster nodded. "What's up, son?"

Mozzie wriggled happily. He was a soft, flabby kid nicknamed for his high-pitched, whining mosquito's voice. "Well, Coach, I was reading the Highwater Junior League Manual last night, and there's a rule in there that says all members of any team must wear an athletic supporter."

Foster looked mystified. "Yes," he agreed. "Are you asking for an inspection, Moz? I think I can trust you boys to know what to put on under your pants."

Blast snickered. "Oh, you can trust us *boys*."

I shot Steven a look. He gazed at Mozzie and Blast, perplexed.

"Oh . . . I see," Foster said. "I guess what you boys are trying to tell me is that some members of this team"—and here he turned to smile at me for the first time, ever—"may not be complying with the letter of Highwater Junior League laws and by-laws. Is that correct?"

"Yeeeeee . . . yeeeee . . ." Mozzie couldn't even squeeze out a "yes." Blast collapsed onto Mozzie's arm and hung there, weak with laughter.

Then I got it. They wanted *me* to wear one. The hinge on my jaw failed.

"Hey," Steven said, "that's not fair!"

Coach Foster smiled. "Sure it is. Rules is rules,

kids. Fran Cullers, if you aren't dressed completely and fully in the uniform required by league rules, I'm afraid that we won't be able to let you continue to play. Unfortunately, we'll have to scratch you from the lineup today." He withdrew the score book from under his arm with a flourish and pulled the pencil from behind his ear.

Billy waved farewell with his bandana.

"I demand to . . . ," I started. But I couldn't demand to see the rule book. I knew it from cover to cover. There was a clause requiring an athletic supporter for every team member, but naturally—I mean, considering nature—I thought I was excluded.

It was going to be a long, discouraging summer.

"Okay, so I'll wear one," I said, my voice sour. Coach Foster looked disappointed until Billy said, "Gee, Fran, I can't let you borrow mine. It's being used. Any of you guys want to lend Fran your jock strap?"

One boy was so overcome he started to hiccup. Two more crumbled to the ground beside Blast, who was now so weak he was lying on the grass laughing. Quoc Nguyen covered his mouth and giggled.

In any other league I would have had the last laugh, because without nine players the Hardwares would have to forfeit. But South Highwater rules let us borrow a player from the other team. He'd be their worst, some guy the Karson Kernels would be happy to dump on us. But just because I'm a girl, the Hardwares would rather have him than me.

"I demand proof that every guy here is wearing a jock strap himself!" I yelled.

"I'll vouch for the team," Foster said, grinning.

"*Visible* proof!" I insisted, but it was useless. I threw down my mitt. Then I pulled off my hat and threw that down, too. I glared at Billy before roasting Mozzie with a long, burning stare.

"EEEEeeeeeeeee." He still couldn't catch his breath.

I stalked away across the diamond. "Hey, it's our turn to warm up," complained the pitcher for the Kernels, but I pushed past him. The center fielder stood aside as I marched across the outfield; it wasn't until I reached the parking lot that the Hardwares' hooting and giggling and gargling and snuffling faded behind me.

I turned the corner of the junior-high school and started to run. Down Bryant Avenue to Alder. Down Alder to Division. I smoked around the corner of Center and flamed down the sidewalk, straight through the open door of Davidson Drugs and Sundries.

"Afternoon." Grey Davidson, old Mr. Davidson's handsome teenage son, glanced up from the magazine he was reading. He looked at my flushed face. "Can I help you, miss?"

"No," I choked. "I'm just here to buy something. Something, uh . . . for my brother." Grey looked at me expectantly. Oh no! I thought. Now he'll wonder if he knows my brother! "Uh, my *little* brother." Grey nodded and smiled. "So I'm going to go look at the boys' stuff," I said. "Is that okay?"

His green eyes, hedged with thick lashes, stared at me.

"Like, men's . . . well . . . boys' . . . underwear."

"Sure, kid. Aisle six. Toward the back." He looked down at his magazine. I stood watching him, trying to catch my breath. Grey looked up again. "You're here to buy, we're here to sell," he said, and smiled. "Store motto."

"Okay." I walked down the candy aisle and pretended to shop for M&M's. When I peeked up at him, Grey smiled.

The bell on the front door tinkled. Someone walked in and Grey turned to help. I hurried down the aisle and tiptoed along the back of the store, turned down aisle six and hustled past fields of women's panties. I sidled over the border into the men's section. I wasn't sure what a jock strap looked like, but I was fairly certain I'd know it when I saw it. On the shelf under the briefs and boxer shorts, kind of hidden away—there they were. Small, medium, and large.

I snatched a package from the shelf. Now I was going to die. I crawled up to the front of the store and slid the package onto the counter.

"Your brother's in Little League?" Grey asked, looking at my uniform.

"Yeah," I lied.

"And you're . . . ?"

"Thirteen. I'm in Junior League," I said, pulling a five-dollar bill out of my pocket; I didn't dare look up.

"That's cool," Grey said and handed me my change. "Go get 'em, kid."

I bounded out the door and rocketed back to the field. Top of the first, I figured, seeing George Andrews at bat.

"I asked for extra-large but they said there wasn't a guy in this town man enough to need one," I snarled as I pulled the jock strap from the bag and waved it at Coach Foster. I was so mad I bit into the package and ripped the plastic off with my teeth; a piece stuck to my tongue. I walked over to the trash can and spat it in. Billy glared at me from second, and Mozzie frowned at me from the dugout. Steven was on first, blushing.

"Eye on the pitch," Foster reminded George, and

then he turned and looked me up and down with his killer's eyes. "You're up next, Cullers," he said. "And you'd better be wearing that thing."

"Oh, good," Billy shouted. "Put it on, Fran!"

"Wearing it," Coach Foster warned grimly as George struck out. I strode toward the batter's box, dangling the cup from its elastic straps in front of me. Halfway to the plate I stopped, turned, and smiled at Foster. I felt like I had in third grade when some kid dared me to peek into the boys' bathroom and I'd surprised a fifth-grader zipping up his pants—like an outlaw.

"What's going on?" a bewildered Karson Kernel asked behind me.

"Hey, Coach?" I asked. "How do you put this on?"

He glared at me. "Quit holding up the damn game, Cullers."

The umpire looked sympathetic. "Well, kid," he said, "put your right leg through one loop and your left leg through the other loop, and hike the whole affair up around your waist."

"Oh, *c'mon*," Steven's mom yelled from the bleachers, but everyone ignored her. The Karson Kernels were laughing now, too.

"Fran, Fran, Fran," Billy sighed. "Now you'll never get a date."

"Is this all it takes?" I asked Foster as I lifted the strap behind my head and wound it around my pony tail. I wouldn't let him take baseball away from me. Life had thrown me some real beanballs lately—fired them straight at my head. Baseball was the one thing I had left.

"Fran . . . ," Foster warned.

I tied the elastic securely in a big bow, then jammed a batting helmet down over my hair. "Wearing it!"

"That's not what the rules say!" Foster bellowed.

"The strap is on her body," the ump said. "Looks legal to me."

Foster shook the wire backstop in frustration.

"What's the count?" I asked.

"One out, man on first and second," the ump said.

I surveyed the Kernels. I knew their pitcher from last year's state All Stars team; he had no tricks up his sleeve, just a hard straight fastball. It'd be easy to drive Billy in from second.

But he'd had his chance. He and the Hardwares— they blew it.

I hailed the third baseman. "Ready?" I called. "This one's yours." He stared at me suspiciously. I stepped to the plate and shot him another smile. "I'm serious; get ready, now." He still didn't believe me and almost didn't catch the easy grounder I smacked his way. He woke up just in time to tag Billy out.

"Now throw it to first!" I suggested. The Karson Kernels stared at me in open-mouthed confusion as I inched in slo-mo toward first base.

Then the pitcher understood. "Double play!" he screamed at the third baseman. "She's *giving* it to us! Throw the ball, man!"

"Franny! What are you doing, Franny?" Steven wailed.

I was destroying the Highwater Hardwares, that's what.

chapter 2

Pinc.

Pinc.

Pinc.

Someone was tossing pebbles against my bedroom window. Shrugging off my sheets, I poked my head outside and inhaled the sweet, grassy morning. Three stories below, Casey Stengel, long dead but still living in my imagination as the manager of Cullers' Classic All Stars, my dream team of all-time greats, grimaced up at me. "Get up, Franny," he said. "That damned old man is pitching. We need you, pronto."

He meant Satchel Paige, of course. I'd tried to recruit Satchel for Cullers' Classic All Stars, but he preferred throwing against us. He said it was more fun. Now the All Stars would need me to save the game. Again.

The back lawn was dewy and cool under my bare feet. There was a mesh bag full of plastic Ping-Pong balls that I kept stashed with a fungo bat under Aunt Beth's lawn chair, and every morning I either pitched or batted one hundred balls against the garage out by the alley.

Whisht—I tossed a plastic ball over my head and—*pop!*—smacked it against the garage while a sleepy-eyed squirrel heckled me from the maple. *Whisht, pop.* Again and again. *Whisht, pop.* Fifty-six. *Whisht-pop.* Fifty-seven. It was an old-fashioned drill that Dad and I used to run together, every day. Now I practiced alone, but Cullers' Classic All Stars kept me motivated.

"Franny!" Far away, over the roar of my imagined crowd, Aunt Beth called.

Ninety-one. Ninety-two.

"Franny! Stop that racket!"

"I'm almost done!"

Time to face Satchel Paige. In my mind I summoned the old Polo Grounds. Satchel had walked Babe Ruth, Hank Aaron, and Joe DiMaggio, three of the best hitters in history, and he'd walked them on purpose. He knew what those clowns were made of—he wanted the girl, he wanted to pitch to Cullers, *she* was the real challenge.

Sweat lathered my palms as I cocked the bat over my shoulder. Satchel had invented so many pitches—submariner, sidearmer, bat dodger, step-n-pitch-it, bee-ball, jump-ball, trouble-ball, long-ball—I'd never seen the same one twice, and he threw them all so fast the ball sometimes evaporated before it reached the plate. True. Now Satchel tape-measured me in a glance, he reared back . . . Strike!

The crowd erupted, screaming insults at me. On third base, Babe passed a hand over his eyes. "Heh-heh," Satchel smirked, and fired again. Strike two!

BOOOOOO!

"Franny!" cried Casey. "You didn't even swing!"

Satchel heard that, and a big "Oh, I get it" grin spread across his face. First pitch, second pitch, that girl didn't even swing! I was playing with him, too. I *wanted* it like this: bottom of the ninth, three runs down, bases loaded, full count, the fierce fireballer versus me, the first girl in professional baseball and already one of the greats.

He nodded; the respect in his eyes couldn't be mistaken. I settled over the plate. I'd thrown away two pitches and now I only had one chance. Could I really do it? Was I tough enough?

I gulped. . . . He reared back. . . . Now!

One hundred.

I tipped my hat to the greatest pitcher of all time and trotted my victory lap. Yeah, I was tough enough. "CUL—LLLLERS!" Fans were scrambling for the home-run ball in the upper tiers of the stadium, and Cullers' Classic All Stars were dancing on home plate. I tagged the maple, the laundry pole, the rusty bumper of Aunt Beth's old Volvo; I vaulted all three steps onto the back porch and tagged Aunt Beth.

She caught me in a headlock. "Shhh! I thought I asked you to be quiet in the morning?"

"Those little balls don't make any noise!"

"But when you imitate the crowd—that's pretty loud." She shook me gently and let me go. "Your dad's finally able to sleep through the night, and now I've got you screaming your own name at five a.m."

"It's almost eight."

"That late? Well, then, I'm lucky you woke up the neighborhood!" Aunt Beth chased me through the back door into the kitchen. I loved living with Aunt Beth. I felt safe here. Coming into the kitchen, I inhaled the smell of warm milk and hot oatmeal.

There was cocoa heating in a pan on the stove, and the newspaper was waiting on the kitchen table. Aunt Beth told me to look in her backpack; she'd picked up the mail from the post office last night. While she rustled in the cabinets and pulled down three big mugs, I flipped through the letters.

"Bill. Bill. Catalogue. Catalogue. Catalogue. And another bill. . . . Look! Here's a check stuck inside a catalogue."

She snatched it from me and cackled. Aunt Beth was a freelance illustrator; most of her work was painting cover illustrations for Torchlight Collections, a line of romance novels. Her studio was in what used to be the living room, and the smell of oil paint sometimes wafted down the hall into the kitchen. Since she wasn't paid steadily, every check was a celebration.

For me there was a postcard from Topanga Canyon Stadium, "the steepest outfield in the minor leagues," and an envelope from Camp Carmichael, a week-long skills camp in New Jersey, the best in the country. I flipped the postcard over first. "How's the arm?" it read. "Still practicing with those plastic golf balls? XOXOXO." The signature was spelled out long: "Sloooooow." That always made me smile.

Jerry "Slow" McGonnagle was my father's best

friend from the summer after high school, when they both played on the Applegate A's, a minor-league team in southern Oregon. Dad went to college, but Slow never left baseball. Now he coached the Topanga Tremors, "a minor team in a minor league so minor no one knows we exist," he said. He sent me goofy postcards from Topanga and from whatever little town he was passing through.

Aunt Beth handed me a mug of hot chocolate. Turpentine fingerprints melted slowly from the blue enamel cup. I showed her the postcard; Slow always made her smile, too. Then she stared some more at her check, and I picked up the envelope from Camp Carmichael.

Crabby Carmichael got the best players in the country to coach at his camp. Dad started sending for the brochures four years ago; every time one came in the mail he would tease me with it, holding it so high above my head I couldn't reach, then he'd read it silently, shake his head, and finally say, "Oh, too bad. We can finally afford to go, and Crabby can only get old fat hacks to coach this summer." Then, fake-sad, he'd read the coaching roster while I screamed in excitement. The plan was, we would take a vacation, just me and Dad: first we'd fly back east for a week at Carmichael's, then we'd drive up to Cooperstown and see the Baseball Hall of Fame, then back down to New York City to watch a real Yankee game. But that was several hundred lifetimes ago. It was before Mom died, before we moved in with Aunt Beth.

I licked the jelly off my knife and slid it under the envelope's flap. Inside was the fall brochure.

Mark McGwire! My Number One Favorite (living, non-Yankee) Pro! He was right there on the cover of the brochure, leaning over a boy my age, guiding the boy's swing, both of them grinning at the camera. I knew Crabby was connected, but Mark McGwire? No way. Maybe it was just a publicity gimmick. I ripped the brochure open and scanned the session descriptions. Way! Mac Attack was going to guest-coach the week of August 18.

"Look, Aunt Beth."

"Who's that?"

"Mark McGwire! He's going to be at Crabby's."

"Mmmmmm." She was a total ditz when it came to baseball, but she wasn't listening to me, anyhow; she was standing in the kitchen doorway, cocking her head up the stairs. "J.J.?" she asked. The only sound was the tick of the cooling stove. "J.J.?"

Tick. Tick.

I stared down at the brochure. I owned a signed

McGwire ball; it was my Number One Favorite (non-Yankee) Possession. Okay, it was better than all the Yankee stuff, too. It was lucky; it made me feel better when I held it, and believe me, I'd held it maybe a million times. Right now it was hidden away in Dad's sock drawer, where I hoped its secret presence would help him feel better, too. I itched to touch it. But to meet McGwire himself, to learn his technique, to actually shake the hand that had signed the ball . . .

"J.J.?" Aunt Beth called again. Sighing, she walked back to the stove and poured the third mug of cocoa. "Here, Fran, go take this to your father. Please make sure he's up. He needs to get down to the shop."

Trying not to let the cocoa slosh out, I crept up the steps to the second floor and baby-stepped down the long hall. At the window, I paused and gazed out at the neighborhood. Over on Fifth Street, outside a messy old house, I saw a moving van. The house next door had new yellow paint and white trim. A lot of people were leaving because they couldn't find jobs, and even when new people moved in and fixed up the houses, I thought the windows looked empty and sad. But Aunt Beth said South Highwater was "up and coming," the perfect place for an artist to snag a big old Victorian before they cost too much.

A little cocoa dribbled on the rug, so I moved slower. I passed the closet that Aunt Beth had given us to store things from our house in Willamette Junction. By the time I got to Dad's door, there wasn't any steam coming out of the mug. I took a big breath and told myself he was better. And when I finally knocked, he answered right away. He was even standing in his bathroom, washing his face, and he turned around and smiled.

Maybe the McGwire Ball had worked.

"Good morning, sunshine," he said, softly.

It hadn't worked. That wasn't his real voice. It was a voice that he'd started using in the last three months, his gentle TV-Dad voice. Still, finding an actor playing my dad was better than finding my real dad sitting on his bed at three in the afternoon, curtains closed, one shoe on, one shoe off, and knowing he'd been stuck like that for hours. I felt silly for having been scared, and I felt bad when he took a sip of the cocoa and frowned.

"Hey, Dad . . ."

He tested his cocoa with a finger. I waited a minute, willing him to look up.

"Dad," I whispered.

"Hmmm?"

I handed him the postcard from Slow. He smiled

again. That made me brave, so I passed him the brochure.

"What's this?" he asked.

"Camp Carmichael."

"Oh yeah. Right."

"Remember?"

He smiled too brightly and nodded.

Excitement made my voice squeak. "Big Mac is going to be there!"

"That's nice, Franny. Maybe next summer."

But what if McGwire doesn't come back to Crabby's next year? If I screamed, would he even hear? Or would he just keep smiling that pleasant smile and staring over my head? I sat down on the bed and sighed. "Okay." Camp Carmichael was a dream that I'd decided a long time ago to live without, so I'd just try and forget about McGwire, too.

I watched Dad comb his hair. Lately, he only shaved every other day. Most of the year he was a mathematics professor at the university over in Willamette Junction, but this summer he was working at a friend's engine-repair shop. Aunt Beth insisted that he get out of the house every day, so each morning he pulled on the same greasy jeans and oily sweatshirt and walked downtown to the garage. Even on Saturday and Sunday.

I got up and went over to the window. Below me, Cullers' Classic All Stars stretched out on the lawn. "Ask him," mouthed Casey.

I already knew the answer, but for Casey's sake I said, "Are you coming to the game tonight, Dad?" If he did, I promised silently, I'd square up and play fair with the Hardwares. I remembered the look on Steven's face when I cost us the last game. I wouldn't want to see the same look on Dad's face.

"We'll see. By the way . . ." I turned around and he handed me the McGwire Ball. "That's very sweet, Franny, but it belongs to you."

It didn't use to belong to me. It belonged to both of us. We found it on eBay. We tracked it for seven days; then, in the final five minutes, Dad threw in a crazy high bid and we won. It cost so much money he said, "Never tell anyone." The deal was, we each got to keep it for a week. We even had a contract and kept track on the calendar. Back then, those several hundred lifetimes ago, Dad would never let me keep the McGwire Ball one millisecond over a week. Now it had been in my possession for more than a year.

But I'm tough, so I just said, "Thanks." Besides, I needed to touch it again. I ran two stairs at a time up to the converted attic, my special bedroom at the top of the house, and, just for old times' sake, I pinned the Camp Carmichael brochure on my wall, next to the others (about ten), and next to the brochures for Cooperstown (six) and the pictures of the Yankees (uncountable). Then I fell backward onto my Yankee beanbag chair and rolled the McGwire Ball over my cheek, up and over the top of my head.

It was after nine now. Maybe I'd walk down to the American Legion field, where a local men's league was starting an early-morning game. Next door, a little girl chanted a skipping-rope song, and somewhere else a lawn mower sputtered, roared, and idled. Like a whisper over these summer sounds was the best summer sound of all: the fans over at the park cheering in a run for the home team.

The seams rolling across my scalp made me feel better. They always do.

The trees outside my window stirred, and the rising breeze carried another cheer. No one cheered for me anymore. No one except the ghostly pals of my own imagination. I closed my eyes. . . . I jogged in from third, my homer a vanishing point on the horizon. Cullers' Classic All Stars swarmed around me, they hugged me in their arms, they lifted me up on their shoulders. Dad waved from the stands. Mom jumped up and down beside him. . . . Mark McGwire was there, too! He pumped his fist in celebration. "I taught her that!" he yelled. . . . I imagined until my heart hurt. I dreamed that those fans were cheering for me.

c h a p t e r   3

Game two in my campaign against the Hardwares.

Hootie Foster pitched so scatter-armed, I wondered if he'd been bribed by the other team. "Let him walk ya, let him walk ya!" The Tasty Town Triple Scoops rolled gum in their chubby cheeks and grinned. Playing for the Triple Scoops was a sweet assignment: free ice cream for a week every time the team won. Motivation was not a problem. They were serious about winning, so serious that they were mean, tricky, and sneaky on the field. But (naturally) slow. This had cost them the last three games. Tonight, their bubblegum-and-chocolate-colored uniforms billowing around their shrinking figures, they were starved for ice cream, salivating for victory.

Hootie's pitch sailed over the backstop.

"You suck!" a Triple Scoop screamed. His teammates clutched their sides and howled. With each wild pitch they tasted Butter Nut Explosion and White Fudge Chunk and Double Brownie Overload.

"He's a little shorter than that, son," Coach Foster snarled.

From left field I watched Hootie sag on the mound. He knew he had no talent. The Hardwares knew it, too. The entire league—the entire *state*—knew he was hopeless. But Hootie was Coach Foster's son, and the coach seemed to think he could intimidate some talent into Hootie.

"Let him walk ya," the Triple Scoops' coach advised his hitter. Like there was any debate.

"Batterbatterbatterbatterbatter," chanted the Hardwares.

"Batterbatter SWING!" yelled Blast as the pitch hit the dirt and rolled toward home plate.

"We're not bowling, Hootie!" Foster screamed. The ump called time out and walked over to conference with the coach. Foster jerked the brim of his cap low over his face. His jaw clenched.

Steven, at first base, caught my eye. Steven was a

little frightened of Coach Foster. He thought Foster, a timberman, had spent too many years in the woods working with chain saws and what Steven called "other weapons of mass destruction." I grinned back at him. After the game with the Karson Kernels he hadn't talked to me for two days, but it looked like he'd thought things through and we were friends again.

I moved in to cover Blast at short. Shortstop used to be my position; it's where I earned my two Golden Gloves. But Foster stuck me in left field, where there wasn't a lot of action. Even though Blast could field pretty well, he was so small—his nickname had been "Tick" before he started blowing up bottles of gasoline in the ravine behind his mother's house—he couldn't reach everything, so he kept me on my toes.

Over Blast's head, I scanned the Hardwares' bleachers. Steven's mother perched on the top bench, her fingers pressed against her lips. Dad was a no-show, not that I'd really expected him. Instead I imagined Cullers' Classic All Stars lining the bottom bench.

"Batterbatterbatter . . ."

Hootie tossed another stinker, but it stayed airborne, so the bored hitter swung anyway and caught a piece of it. I ran up to cover Blast, but he snagged the ball, spun three times, and threw to Billy at third.

"FIRST, DUMMY!" Foster shouted. The play was

backwards but, luckily for the Hardwares, Billy had a smoking fast arm.

"OW!" Steven yelped. "Ease up a little, Billy, I almost dropped it!"

"Six runs that inning," spat Foster as we trotted in. "I can't believe this—" Nearby, the ump cleared his throat. Foster shot the man a look, sighed, and checked his clipboard. "Oh, criminy. Mozzie, you're up."

As everyone else shambled around, I darted toward the dugout. If I got there first, it was mine to enjoy alone. Only Steven would share the same bench, and he was already holding it down. He waved me in.

"You know those guys who hole up in their house, then go berserk and shoot people?" he asked as I plopped down beside him.

"Yeah?"

"Well, I heard Foster was laid off last year. He's alone all day at home. Hootie says he just . . . broods." Holding his finger out like a gun, Steven cocked his thumb and popped off some imaginary rounds toward the infield.

Billy poked his head around the door frame. "Girl germs," he muttered and stalked off. Angel Diaz smacked the door frame and followed Billy, then Blast looked in and made a rude noise. I sighed. MacKenzie Wheeler sauntered back from the Goodie Wagon with a tray full of sodas; her reception was so enthusiastic, I could only figure she had the right kind of germs.

"Swing, damn it!" Foster screamed. Mozzie hunched his shoulders and dug in over the plate.

"No, son," the ump said kindly. "That was the third strike. You're out."

Another figure darkened the doorway, but now it was Steven's mother with orange Gatorade. Parents were supposed to stay out of the dugout, but Mrs. Chauppette ignored that rule. All game long she was at it, ferrying water, ChapStick, GU, Handy Wipes, PowerBars, Tiger Balm, and whatever else Steven's heart desired back and forth from the bleachers to her son. She was like a busy bird with a nest. Now she half-lowered herself onto the bench beside Steven, but jumped back up at the last moment and saved her white shorts. She looked the way MacKenzie was going to look when she grew up: perfect.

"How is that handsome father of yours, Francine?"

I couldn't unpry my lips. "Mmm."

"Well, you just tell him 'Hi' for me, won't you?"

"Mmmmmmm."

"We just don't see him enough around here anymore, you know," she continued. "And how are you getting along, Miss Blondie? How I wish I had thick yellow hair like yours, you pretty little thing."

Steven snickered. As soon as Mama Bird flew away I would deal with that. I knew her compliments weren't true. Mrs. Chauppette had gone to college with Mom and Dad, and she thought she knew all our business. She felt sorry for me. "Do you need anything else, Steven?" He eyed his loot and considered. "No? Okay, good luck, you two." It'd been an eternity, but she finally backed out of the dugout, yelling, "Here we go! Here we go! C'mon, Hardwares!" and clapping her hands.

Steven grinned as she bounced away. "Little Miss Blondie," he mimicked.

"Hey, Steven. What's that around your wrist?" I pointed to a ratty braided string he'd been wearing since he moved back from California. It looked ridiculous and I was a little embarrassed for him, so I'd kept mum about it up to now.

"My dad gave it to me. The guys on the beach wear them."

"Looks like a sissy bracelet to me."

His eyes narrowed. "That's 'cuz you're not hip, Little Miss Blondie."

I nodded at another raggedy surfer string tied around his ankle. "And that—another girlie bracelet?"

"Little Miss Bl—" He felt my elbow in his ribs.

"Sissy."

Wisely, he let it drop. "Hey, look," he said, pointing across the field. Over on another diamond the Foursquare Flyers, the best team in the league, covered their positions like pros; their bleachers were rocking with dancing fans, and someone started the Wave. "We're playing them in a few weeks."

I hummed a funeral dirge.

"What's with you, Fran? When we were with the Rosewood Baggers, you couldn't wait to take on the good teams."

"That's because we *were* a good team, Steven."

"The Hardwares are a good team, too. Or we could be. We're on the team, aren't we? Billy's good. Angel and George have some talent. If we could only get everyone to pull togeth—"

I was pointing at the jock strap. Today I wore it around my neck like a noose.

He flushed. "They're only joking, Fran. We're still a team."

I snorted. "Tell that to Billy Smythe. Tell that to Coach Foster." I held my finger out like Steven's pretend gun. "I can't believe you defend those punks."

"You're making it worse than it needs to be! Giving that double play to the Kernels last game— that was really wrong."

Quoc popped a fly out over the infield, but the

Triple Scoop shortstop just camped out under it and waved it into his mitt.

"Cullers," Foster moaned.

I jumped up and glared at Steven. *I* was making it worse? I didn't need a sermon.

"C'mon, Franny. Enough's enough. Play fair, promise me."

"Go, Franny!" Mrs. Chauppette called as I tramped up to the plate.

The catcher handed me my bat with mock courtesy. "I like your sense of style," he smirked, pointing at the jock strap. "Very girlie."

"Got any girls on *your* team?"

"Nah." His nasty smile was fenced in behind the metal gate of his mask. "We don't need any crybabies on this team."

What *was* with this town? There was just no relief. So, while visions of Peanut Butter Chocolate Swirl dripped in the daydreams of the drooling Triple Scoops, I stepped into the first pitch and blasted it out over the pitcher's head so hard and fast I swear I saw his hair blow back as he ducked.

"GO GO GO!!!" screamed the Hardwares. For a minute we were all teammates as I sprinted around first base and then to second. The Hardwares were rooting for *me!* I streaked toward third and saw that even MacKenzie, Tiffany, and Selena were kicking their legs in one of their silly cheers.

The bullet from left field was a white blur in the corner of my right eye; I folded my left leg and slid into third base not one second before I heard the thud of ball striking mitt.

"Spike!" The third baseman gripped his leg and screamed.

"Spike!" wailed the Triple Scoop coach, waving his arms in horror. "Spike!"

"No way!" I stared up at the blubbering boy. He clutched his foot dramatically, but his quaking cheeks were dry and his pupils pinpricks.

Ice cream. It was all about the ice cream.

"C'mon!" I said. "You were at least two feet from the bag!"

He squeezed his pink lids over his crafty eyes. "Spike," he whimpered.

"Spiiiiiike!"

I lifted my head from the dirt and watched a woman stagger from her seat in the bleachers, falter, and fall sideways into the arms of the mothers around her. "Jackson!" she cried.

The infield ump strode over to third. Coach Foster

looked confused—he knew I was capable of a spike, but he was probably surprised that I'd use it on someone outside the Hardwares.

"I said 'safe,' " the ump yelled. "C'mon, kid—those cleats are only rubber. Take it like a man."

I ran my tongue along my gritty teeth, scrambled to my feet, and shook the chalk out of my ponytail. "I thought you didn't want crybabies on your team," I yelled at the catcher. Over his head, Jackson's mother waved a threatening finger at me.

"Batter up!"

Steven strode over to the plate, puffing his chest out like a superhero. He took a practice swing, looked up, and caught my eye. He stared at me. It took me a minute to realize what he was doing: asking a question. Was I for him or against him? Would I play fair?

I found a pebble in my mouth and spat. So like Steven, I thought bitterly. All these bad guys picking on me, but did he notice? Did he fly to my rescue? No. He was still wagging his finger and lecturing on fair play.

I pointed at the jock strap. I shook my head.

"Batterbatterbatter!" chattered the Triple Scoops. The catcher's teeth moved behind his mask.

Steven stepped into the box. *Chunk!* He steamed

for first. But the fielders were empty-handed while the catcher scrambled in the dirt. It took me a second to understand.

Steven was a solid slugger. He could have powered a hit into right field and landed safely on first while I ran home. But he made a bad bunt—he laid the ball right at the catcher's feet. For the team's sake I should have stayed put, because on a bunt like that I was a sure out.

It was a *dare.* He asked me a question and I said no, so now he was daring me to play fair. He gave me a play I could screw up. Well, I was going to get back at the Hardwares, and goody-goody Steven couldn't stop me.

I ran.

"NOOOO!" Foster screamed, but I ran—straight into the arms of the catcher, who embraced me with one arm and with the other hand, the hand with the ball, socked me in the gut.

I clutched my stomach and dropped to the plate on my knees. "Don't cry, girlie," the catcher hissed. *Huc, huc . . .* I gasped . . . my lungs flat . . . *huuuuuc . . .* I knew I was going to live when I tasted the catcher's sweat on my lips.

I staggered to my feet and waded through the

changing tide of leaping Triple Scoops and dragging Hardwares as they switched places on the field. Jackson's mother was still glaring at me, but nobody came to *my* defense.

"Nice going, stupid," Billy jeered.

Mrs. Chauppette clutched the fence. "Fran, are you okay?"

"Yeah." I snatched my mitt. Go away, I thought. You're not my mother.

I limped past Steven. He wouldn't look at me. "Nice bunt," I said, and swatted his arm. "Thanks." He jerked his arm away.

The Triple Scoops knew they had us now. Coach Foster squeezed his arms over his chest and screamed instructions at Hootie, who threw almost everywhere but over the plate. A Triple Scoop dribbled the ball back into the infield, where George and Blast both raced after it and collided in a cartwheel of dust and curses.

We were going to lose anyway. I just gave the events a little nudge.

"Steven," I called. He wouldn't look at me.

I looked at the parents in the bleachers. I tried to imagine Cullers' Classic All Stars lined along the bottom bench again, but right now even they had deserted me.

"Heads up in left field!" Coach Foster yelled.

I saw it. It spun toward me slow—the kind of catch everyone likes, the kind that plops down soft into your mitt like it's just practice. I raised my mitt against the sky, but I'd have to take three steps to the right to reach the ball.

So I just stood there.

Fran Cullers, 2. Highwater Hardwares, 0.

chapter 4

This is why I like Steven: he gets over things fast. Already he didn't care about me running on the bunt. In fact, he put his arm around my shoulder and drew me into the team huddle.

"Two, four, six, eight, who do we appreciate? Triple Scoops . . ." We launched our mitts skywards. Then Billy hawked up a big mouthful of spit and landed it square on my right toe.

"YAAAAAA!" screamed the Triple Scoops as they stampeded toward the parking lot: finally, ice cream.

"You—" I lunged for Billy. Steven held me back. I fought him, but he had me firmly by the shoulders.

He forced me around and steered me away from the team.

"Two, four, six, eight, who'd we like to *exterminate*," Billy jeered. "FRAN!"

"Ow, Steven. Let me go!" I scuffed my cleats through the dirt, trying to dry the spit mark. My toes curled in disgust.

"I didn't know Slow McGonnagle was in town," Steven remarked.

"He's not." Yuck. I knew I couldn't ask Dad to buy me new Adidas, but these felt forever ruined. It wasn't just the spit. It was the disgusting essence of Billy. Boy germs.

Steven didn't appear to be impressed by my problem. He was still nattering on about Slow. "Oh, really?" he said. "Then how come he's been watching us for the entire game, from over there?" Steven was pointing toward the adjoining field.

"That can't be—" I started to follow his finger . . . and then I caught myself. Don't look, I thought. Steven never lies. He's too righteous.

His eyes were small and hard. "I saw Slow and your dad walking across the field. So I made that bunt. And when you ran into it . . ."

My blood chilled. Steven knew I wouldn't have

misbehaved if I'd realized Slow was watching. He'd tricked me. Was it puberty? When had Steven developed this mean streak?

"...they stopped," he continued. "Dead in their tracks. Then they went over there"—Steven pointed again—"and watched the rest of the game from the Flyers' bleachers."

I'm not going to look, I told myself. Don't look.

Steven slapped my arm, just like I had slapped his after the bunt. "Nice catch in that last inning," he mocked. "I bet Slow thought so, too."

I'm going to walk across the infield, I thought, and get my bike and pedal off, and pretend that Steven is lying. If he's learned to be this mean, he's probably also learned to lie. I suggested as much. "You're lying," I said. The right side of his mouth jerked upward in a grim smile.

"You're lying!"

Billy waited for me by the backstop, his hands on his hips, bubbling more spit out of the corner of his mouth. I escaped him by dodging around the opposite corner of the fence and mixing with the game's stragglers. Coach Foster, his arms crossed and his face blotched, was engaged in an angry discussion with the ump. "He's my son and I'll raise him how I want," he snarled.

Finally, Billy lost interest and strolled over to join the Three Most Popular Girls over at the Goodie Wagon. Play it cool, I thought. Don't let Steven know he rattled you. I sauntered toward my bike, yet, despite myself, my ears strained for the sound of my name floating from the far field. But . . . Steven was lying. I knew he was! I didn't understand my dad at all, lately, but Slow McGonnagle was my biggest fan. He wouldn't watch my game from another team's bleachers, unless . . .

"Franny!" My heart somersaulted in my chest before I realized the voice wasn't Slow's. Mrs. Chauppette said, "Do you need a ride, honey?"

Slowly, casually, hoping Steven wouldn't notice my hands were trembling, I picked my bike up and peeked over my shoulder. I noticed that the rec department had had to drag in an extra bleacher for the game; up and down the boards, Flyers and Flyer fans danced a victory jig.

There—moving toward the parking lot. Slow's fire-colored thatch burned against the blue sky.

"No thanks. Gotta go," I gargled.

"Thought so," Steven said.

• • •

Sooner or later, I had to go home.

But first I wasted some time. I rode down to the

river and washed the spat-on shoe in the water. A lot of topics were clamoring for my attention, but I tried to ignore my crowded mind. I concentrated on scrubbing the spit out with sand. Then I washed the other shoe, so that they'd look the same. I put them on a rock and waited for them to dry, though there really wasn't enough time before the sun set.

River water squished between my toes as I wheeled my bike up the drive.

Slow's old Ford pickup was plastered with decals of major- and minor-league teams, some new since his last visit, others weathered and peeling. I slipped my finger along its side and traced a line through the grime of—how many states? He liked to surprise us with his visits. He said it was his way of ignoring the distance that separated him from his best friend, my dad. He liked to pretend that he lived right next door, and that he could just pop in without calling.

I remembered three years ago after one of Slow's surprise visits. My father and I sat in the backyard on the grass, oiling our mitts. He told me how he had loved playing ball that summer after high school, but when the summer ended, his life went one way, and Slow's another. "It's better to have a real job. You can't get old in baseball. Your body wears out. If you don't make the majors, if you spend all your best years kicking around in the minors, then what are you good for?" He sounded like he was trying to convince himself. "No, at that point there's nothing left except memories of the glory days. Those memories can't feed a family."

But that wasn't Slow's philosophy. The game was supporting him just fine. He loved everything about his life: the crowded bus rattling from one small town to the next ("Small-town America looks all the same, Franny—like Heaven"); the shabby motel rooms ("Just imagine, Fran—I never have to make my own bed"); the familiar faces at every hometown game ("Tremors fans are the most optimistic people in the world"). Most of all, he loved the minors: no megawatt lights and plastic AstroTurf like the bigs, just baseball played the way the game is supposed to be played, on hometown fields parched by drought, dust swallowing a long slide into home plate, barefisted fights when a shortsighted ump makes a lousy call, some stranger, a sweet-scented woman, carrying over a Coke to soothe your throat. . . .

"Whoa!" Dad always stopped Slow before the stories got even more interesting. "Let's remember there's a kid in the room."

My finger stopped at the headlight. Baseball, in any league I could make it—that was the life for me.

Someday I'd break the sex barrier, just like Jackie Robinson broke the color barrier. My battle against the Hardwares was just toughening me up for the long fight ahead. Surely Slow would understand.

I slipped my shoes off on the back porch and draped the jock strap over them. As I stepped into the hallway I could hear Aunt Beth giggling in the kitchen. My father laughed weakly, like he couldn't quite remember how, and then Slow's voice swelled down the hall like Dolby Surround Sound Stereo.

"WELL, look at that BEANPOLE! What ya raising here, John? A BASKETBALL player?" Slow McGonnagle burst out of the kitchen and engulfed me in his big, sunburned arms. He squeezed me so hard I thought my ribs would break—oh, I didn't mind. I closed my eyes and, with my nose squashed into his chest, sucked him all in: sweat, chalk, grass. "Scrape your head on any BACKSTOPS lately, kid?" His voice boomed up through his chest and hummed through me like a current, and something inside me relaxed. He wasn't mad, I just knew he wasn't. He rubbed my head with his knuckles. "Why are your feet wet?"

"Long story."

"Sit down! Sit down!" Aunt Beth shooed us apart and into our chairs around the kitchen table. "Isn't this a great surprise, Franny? Where have you been? We've been waiting forever for you!"

"It's our lucky day, Fran," my dad said. He peered up at me sideways. "Beth actually cooked."

"Hey, hey," Aunt Beth chided, "the stove's an equal-opportunity implement, you know."

Slow relaxed something in everybody, it seemed. Aunt Beth giggled more, and even my father looked happy in a real way. Kind of.

"Oh, J.J. can cook," Slow bellowed. "What's that dish you always made when we were on the road? Hot-dog-and-creamed-corn casserole?"

"Haute cuisine!" Dad said.

"Not when you just dumped the ingredients in a bowl and refused to heat it."

"Well . . . as I remember, we didn't always have access to a stove."

Slow laughed. He wasn't handsome; his face was as rough and lumpy as a burlap bag full of potatoes, and his small blue eyes were crowded between his nose and his big cheeks. He patted his belly. "I think I'll stick with your sister's famous artichoke pie." They didn't seem mad; in fact, everything felt pretty chummy. Excellent. To celebrate, I served myself another helping of artichoke pie.

"So I hear the Hardwares are having a slow season," Aunt Beth said. "Are they in some sort of a slump?"

I hoped that someone here knew the Heimlich maneuver, because I was going to choke on a big lump of artichoke.

"Yeah," Dad said, "I hear that the Hardwares seem to lack team spirit. And spirit's an essential ingredient. Absolutely essential."

I would have asked, "Where did you hear that?" but I was still gagging on the artichoke. Why didn't they just admit they were at the game today?

Aunt Beth got up to pour me a glass of water. "The kids had a lot of team spirit over in Willamette Junction, didn't they? Maybe they just had more going for them in life, you know?"

Slow blew air around a mouthful of pie. "Hell," he said, swallowing. "Some of the greatest players come from the most reduced circumstances. Poverty makes 'em tough. Gives 'em drive. But South Highwater ain't exactly a slum."

"Maybe it's their age, then," Dad tried. "Maybe they're all going through a stage."

How much had they seen?! Well, it didn't sound like they blamed me for anything, that was a relief. "Coach Foster isn't that swift," I suggested. "He yells at us a lot. It's hard to rally around him, you know?"

"Hmmmm." Even Aunt Beth, until now only concerned with keeping her giggles contained, caught the warning rumble. "Hmmmmm," Slow said again, like a volcano moving around inside itself. "Never took much stock in blaming the coach, Fran. Especially now that I'm coaching and I know how tough it is to motivate a bunch of selfish crybabies to work together as a real team. They expect me to motivate them, but who motivates *me*? Hmmmm . . ." Slow's cheeks creased up around his eyes. He stared at me. "Who motivates the *coach*?"

"The idea of team motivates the coach," my dad volunteered.

"That's right—I thought you'd forgot that." Slow fixed Dad with his hard-eyed stare. My father scratched his ear. He looked uncomfortable, like the hotshot kid in class who shouts out an answer but isn't prepared for the exam.

"Well . . . that was a long time ago."

"Not so long ago," Slow contradicted. "Didn't you coach Franny's team over in Willamette?" Dad mashed a piece of pie crust under his fork, then stared at the result. Slow said, "Your dad was a good coach, wasn't he, Fran?"

"Yup."

"Should have had my job. Great eye for hidden

talent. Always knew how to motivate the guys—remember when you helped me out of that tight spot?"

Dad sighed and looked up. For some reason Slow was mad at him (not me!), but now it blew over. "Tight spot? You owe your career to me, Slow. That manager was ready to kick you off the team. He ordered you to lose twenty pounds by the end of the month, and what do you do? You just ate and ate and ate." They laughed. "But you hid everything so no one knew. Bags of potato chips under the bed, boxes of candy bars in the trunk of your car."

"I was *worried*," Slow protested. "I always eat when I'm worried."

"You gained twenty more pounds!"

"I guess I'm just a man who likes to feel padded. But on the twentieth day, Fran, your dad had his big idea." As if I didn't know. As if I couldn't move my lips to the well-remembered words. "I'm sittin' in a café lickin' the last of some fudge off my spoon. I'd been comforting myself with hot-fudge sundaes, see. Lots of them. I'm slurpin' this one down, fending off the flies. J.J. walks in, and before I could stop him, he intercepts the waitress bringin' me my bill."

Dad pretended he was looking at that bill again. "*Nineteen* hot-fudge sundaes!"

"He sits down and just shakes his head," Slow continued. "But then the puddle of recently deceased flies I have stacked over by the sugar shaker catches his eye. 'You're the one dispatching all these insects?' he asks me. 'You may be fat, but you're fast, my friend. Maybe there's something we can do with that.' "

Aunt Beth giggled. She'd heard this story over and over, too, but she loved it as much as I did. Dad smiled and leaned back in his chair.

"Hell, I knew I was fast," Slow said. "Never was a creepy-crawly that could get away with a mouthful of my dessert. And I knew that I was fast on the field, too. Some of the biggest animals on this earth—bulls, elephants, alligators—"

"Bulls, elephants, alligators," I whispered in sync.

"—they get their legs rollin' and, brother, they can hustle. So J.J. suggests that I just strut my stuff, see, and next game I'm stealing bases like they're gold and I'm Jesse James, but I don't need a horse like a regular outlaw—I got horsepower in my legs. And that manager, he sees me take those bases, and he sees those basemen cowering behind their gloves, and he knows that speed is only half of the equation. He knows no man wants to block a base against me. Kind of like facing down a steamroller, he decides. I never heard another word about my, er, 'handicap.' The only word that ever came down from management was my new nickname. 'Slow.' "

We all laughed. Sure, we knew the story, but Slow's delight refreshed all the familiar parts. I wished I had stories that could make my dad smile the way he was smiling right now. "Hey, Dad," I could say, "want to hear about the one where I ran home on a bunt? It really made the right people mad. . . ."

"Coffee?" Aunt Beth asked. "I can make it iced."

"I'll get it," my father said, scraping his chair back. "Let's have your pudding out on the back porch, where it's a bit cooler."

I was still holding my breath a little, but now I could relax. It looked as if there'd be no hard questions about my game today. Now Slow and my father would pass the old stories back and forth between them like old photographs dug out of a trunk in the attic, staring in their mind's eye at old faces like half-forgotten relatives in an ancient album, until Slow or my dad said, "Oh I remember him. . . ." I would watch the moths pelt the porch light and drowse to the lullaby of "remember this" and "remember that."

"Leave the dishes until tomorrow," Aunt Beth whispered, so while my father ground the coffee beans I slipped out the back door and waded across the warm grass to the back fence. I needed a minute alone. The suburban lights milked the night sky of most of its stars, but tonight as I tipped my head back and looked for the tiny lights salted across the black, I saw one shine brightly through the haze. A planet, probably. I wondered if you could wish on a planet like you could wish on a star.

"Planet light, planet bright, first planet that I see tonight. . . ." It didn't sound right, but I wished on it anyway.

chapter 5

"Think fast!"

I whirled just in time to catch the ball that streaked across the yard. "Ow!" I dropped it.

"Caught it with your left hand, and in the dark," Slow observed as he slipped from the shadows of the back porch. "You need a mitt, but your instincts are dead on. Pretty good, Fran. Pretty good for a kid that couldn't handle a fly today."

The baseball glowed in the soft, milky light from the street lamp at the end of the alleyway. As Slow ambled over the lawn, the crickets stopped chirping. My heart stopped for a second, too.

"Thought maybe you needed some coaching," he

said, stepping under the elm. "But it doesn't look like there's a thing wrong. Nothing that a little attitude adjustment won't fix."

"So you admit that you were there today?"

"Yeah, we were there. I can't believe what I saw! That was a bad bunt. The catcher had the ball before you left third—why did you run? And you didn't miss that fly by mistake, Franny. Your dad thinks it was a mistake, but he's wrong. It was too easy. You're too good. What's going on?"

I shrugged and watched my aunt and my father as they passed back and forth in the brightly lit kitchen. Dad tried to take down the promotional Mariner mugs he'd collected from a burger joint; Aunt Beth scolded, and he hunched his shoulders and replaced the cups on the shelf.

"Nothing's wrong," I said. "I was distracted—the sun was in my eyes. It happens sometimes."

"Yeah, it happens sometimes, but not when the sun is *behind* you," Slow growled. "It happens sometimes, but not to a kid who can catch a ball in the dark. You have a special instinct, honey. It doesn't happen to *you*."

I could tell Slow was really warming up. Give him the slightest reason, and he'd launch into something that sounded a lot like a dugout pep talk. The kind you get bottom of the seventh, scoreboard stacked against the team, guys losing focus and bungling the game. Usually, I loved to listen to him. But tonight, I could tell, I was the player making all the errors.

"Nothing's wrong," I croaked. Slow just stared at me. "Okay," I said and shrugged, "so my game has been a little off lately."

The elm leaves drifted in a faint breeze and dappled Slow's face with shadows; he put his hands in his jeans pockets and stared at me some more. I guess a good coach knows when to preach, and when to use the silent treatment.

I tried to out-quiet him.

I gave up.

"I'm just a girl," I shouted. "I can't play pro ball. I'll have to give it up anyway, so who cares if my game is off? Why does it matter?"

I picked up the baseball and fired it to Slow. He hurtled it back. "It matters, Fran. It's not about future glory—it's about today. It's about doing your best, no matter what kind of player you are—skinny or fat, fast or slow, good or bad, boy or girl."

I thought of Coach Foster. How he hated me for no reason whatsoever. How the sheriff had to come and talk to him before I was allowed to play—Slow knew the story. I reminded him of it now. Still, he shook his head at me. He sided with Foster! "That man's under a lot of pressure, Fran. The entire logging industry, a whole way of life, died here. Life changed the rules on Mr. Foster, and he's bitter about it. Men act funny when they can't get a job. But that doesn't excuse you. You can't let your team down."

"My team! Do you have any idea what kind of boys are on my team?"

"I don't care if they're all convicts out on work release—if you let them down like you did today, then you're no better than they are."

"What about me? They're all out to get me!" I thought of the jock strap, of Billy spitting on my shoe. "They hate me because I'm a girl. And better than they are. So I'm showing them. That's all."

"*Showing* them?" He stared at me. "Is that what you're playing ball for? Equal opportunity? One name: Jackie Robinson. Know him?"

Oh, jeez, I thought. Now it really begins. When Slow brought up a famous player, there was always a lesson attached.

"Know him?" Slow insisted. I crossed my arms and stared out over the fence. "Well, if you're not going to answer, let me refresh your memory: first black man in the major leagues. The major *white* leagues. You know what they called him, Fran? 'Nigger. Coon.

Jungle bunny.' Not just the opposing players. Not just the spectators. His own *teammates,* Fran.

"Baseball's not a nice place. There's a lot of meanness in the dugout. A lot of jealousy, a lot of spite, a lot of prejudice. Insults, profanity—black eyes, fistfights. But how did Jackie's story go? You ever hear of Jackie muffing a fly over hurt feelings? How did Jackie 'show' his team? DIGNITY."

I seethed. This was just not fair. Of course I knew Jackie's story! He was an honored member of Cullers' Classic All Stars, and I did not like having him used against me like this.

"A team's not about liking each other. It's not about holding hands and slumber parties with your best friends. A team's about winning baseball games. Everyone does their part—with the other guys, despite the other guys. Jackie understood that. That man was a true champ. It's so basic, I'm surprised I have to spell it out for you. You used to be a great player, Fran—and I'm not talking about physical skill. You used to have the heart of a champ, too."

"Used to." I almost choked on those dry words. "Lots of things used to be." My father used to talk to me, not avoid me. Used to coach my team. Used to practice with me, every day, used to catch one hundred pitches, used to turn around and pitch me one hundred balls.

"Yeah," Slow said. "Used to make me think I should go out and get hitched just so I could have a kid like you. You taught me it wasn't where you went with your talent—it wasn't the majors and contracts and limos that made you a success—it was the heart you brought to the game. How much you loved baseball. Made me feel better about myself and the way I never was good enough for the bigs. Yeah, used to want a little girl just like you."

The elm tossed its leaves in a sudden breeze, and Slow's eyes flashed in the lamplight from the alley. "Fran, the world's changing, and there may well be women in pro ball soon. But they're only going to draft team players, because it's a team sport."

There were a million comebacks to that; helplessly, I realized I wouldn't think of any until tomorrow.

"Ten seasons—that's how long Robinson endured. Would have gone longer if he'd been younger when they let him in. Ten seasons . . . but he made it to the final inning. You know when the ump comes out and declares the start of the game? He says, 'Play ball.' He doesn't say, 'Work out your personal grudges.' That's what it's about: playing your best, nine innings, straight and true. You don't factor anything else in—you just play *ball*, all the way through to the final inning."

Slow was too good. He had hundreds, maybe thousands of locker-room speeches under his belt. He'd probably been using this very same speech for years; I imagined the guys on the Topanga Tremors slapping their foreheads and groaning, "Oh no, it's the 'Jackie played honorably until the final inning' speech!" On the face of it, Slow was right. But sometimes the player knows where the game is headed, no matter what the coach says. The players are on the field, and the coach is only a poet watching from the sidelines. Still, my words were no match for Slow's. All I could say was, "You don't understand."

The back door whacked as Aunt Beth slipped out onto the porch. "Slow? Fran? Pudding and coffee are ready."

"We used to understand each other, kid. And I think we still do." Slow's head rustled the leaves as he moved out from under the tree. His voice was soft, but his words slapped me across the face:

"There's nothing wrong with your game. But I was wrong about your heart—you're no champion."

c h a p t e r 6

NO CHAMPION.

I ran straight up to my room, and no one called me down for pudding. Facedown in my pillow, I listened to the voices on the back porch. They were low and quiet, whispering, not the easy back-and-forth of glory-day "remember this" and "remember that." Slow was working on my father now. ". . . The final inning . . ." Was he still at it? Then I thought I heard my name cutting through the whine of mosquitoes and the thump of June bugs against the window screen. "Fran . . . yeah . . . sure NO CHAMPION."

I woke up the next morning holding the McGwire Ball. Only its comforting seams rolling across my head had put me to sleep. A morning breeze played with the posters that papered my bedroom walls. Cullers' Classic All Stars—Pete Rose, Roger Maris, Joe DiMaggio, Mickey Mantle, Reggie Jackson, Johnny Bench, Sandy Koufax, Bob Gibson, Babe Ruth, Willie Mays, Honus Wagner, Lou Gehrig, Roberto Clemente, and Hank Aaron—usually their eyes followed me everywhere, but today they refused to come to life and talk to me. The poster of the last All Star, Jackie Robinson, was pinned behind my headboard. I couldn't look.

No one, not even Slow, could make me cry.

I waited in my bedroom until I heard him leave. The pickup door slammed, the engine coughed, Slow puttered away. Gone without a good-bye. A few minutes later, Dad's footsteps went downstairs and the front door closed.

The kitchen sink was littered with toast crusts and coffee grits. Someone had washed the dinner and breakfast dishes. Slow's plate, my father's, Aunt Beth's, mine: each clean surface reflected my blurred portrait as I picked a cereal bowl from the drying rack. My distorted features stared back at me from the bottom of the bowl; I moved the milky mirror so that my nose elongated, then shrank, my forehead bloated, then narrowed, my cheeks ballooned 'and my chin stretched: the ugly face of a girl who could never be a champion.

So? What did that make me? Slow hadn't said, but, the way he'd looked at me, I felt like swamp spawn, a lagoon monster who dragged its slimy belly through the dirt after dark, hunting for little kids to eat.

"Fran?" Aunt Beth called from her studio. "I made some cookies. If you hurry you can grab a couple before I inhale the rest."

I sighed and put the bowl back in the rack. Abandoned by my father, insulted by his friend, raised by an aunt who fed me sugar for breakfast—no wonder I was a criminal.

• • •

"There's no cereal?"

"Slow ate it all. The cookies are under the sink," Aunt Beth said. "And bring me a few more, okay? Or just bring in the jar."

"I know about that under-the-sink hiding place," I informed her as I carried the cookies into her studio.

"Sure you do," she said. "But does your dad? Your grandma used to bake goodies and hide them in his closet so that he could eat them before I found them.

Now it's payback time." She grinned at me over a chocolate-chip cookie. "Are you okay? You're late this morning."

"Yeah. Fine," I mumbled. Just fine for an anti-champ, I thought.

Daintily, Aunt Beth touched each fingertip with her tongue, then picked up a brush and nudged a chocolate crumb from a blue puddle on her palette. Magazine photos and pencil sketches fanned across her worktable; in the middle of that mess, Aunt Beth worked on a loose watercolor. A young man in breeches and gold-buckled shoes squinted up off the paper; with his white shirt, wide collar, and long ponytail, he looked like a Pilgrim, but the paisley scarf knotted around his waist looked too jaunty for a stern-faced Puritan. His eyes glinted devilishly.

"Is he a pirate?" I asked.

Aunt Beth smiled. "Yes, *she* is." She dabbed in a small shadow that hinted at the young pirate's sex. "It's for a book about Mary Read. She was raised as a boy and joined the merchant marines in 1700. When the ship was captured by pirates, she signed on with the bad guys." Beth's brush swept a strand of hair across Mary Read's forehead.

Loose thoughts frisked around my mind, but I

couldn't lasso any long enough to figure out why I was so intrigued. "No one guessed?"

Aunt Beth shook her head. "Well, not until she fell in love with a shipmate. *He* guessed. There's a biography over on the desk. Right on top of Torchlight Collections' brilliant new romance, a *fictionalized* account of Mary's life. Get this: Mary has 'deep eyes that made a man think about things he'd not admit to the rough crowd around the galley table.' HA! What crap."

"Is this the book?" It appeared to have spent the last fifty years in the library stacks under a leaky ceiling. There were no illustrations or photos inside. "How'd she do it?" I asked, trying to sound casual.

"Hmmmmm?" Aunt Beth frowned down at her painting.

"How'd she pass herself off as a man?"

Aunt Beth sighed and swept some cookie crumbs off her board. "Oh, women used to do that all the time, honey. I guess they cut their hair and bound their chests with dish towels or something. Don't ask me why no one noticed they didn't need to shave. Some women even joined the Revolutionary War dressed like men, the Civil War, too, and Mary Read wasn't the only female pirate, you know."

I hadn't known. I flipped through the biography, but the words were lifeless. I peeked at the Torchlight Collections manuscript, too, but on page three Mary Read "squelched a girlish giggle," and I dropped it. Only Aunt Beth's sketch seemed to tell me what I needed to know; the lines and shadows hinted man, then woman, then man, then woman again. Like a feather, Mary Read tickled my mind. . . . Why?

Maybe because she loved something as much as I loved baseball. How old was she, I wondered, when she first tasted salty air, first saw the gulls wheeling over water, first walked across a ship deck and knew she was home? Was she six, the same age that I was when I first scuffled across a baseball diamond? Only no one ever told Mary Read she couldn't be a pirate because she was a girl, because no one ever knew she *was* a girl.

And that's when it hit me. My vision of my future: me without a ponytail, me in baggy jeans, a hooded sweatshirt, black high-tops—boy's clothes. Me keeping my voice low, swearing a lot, spitting, making fun of girls. Well, maybe I couldn't go that far. The rest was easy, though. No one would suspect. I'd be . . . *Frank.*

"Thinking pretty hard, huh?" Aunt Beth asked.

I jumped. "Oh . . . no." But, yes, I'd been far away,

walking down a road with Frank Cullers, a road that I could map better with each passing minute. I grabbed another cookie. "Thanks, Aunt Beth."

"You're welcome, but don't forget, those cookies are our secret, okay?" she said. I didn't answer because I was running up the stairs two at a time. I burst into the second-floor bathroom and stared at my reflection in the toothpaste-smeared mirror that for the last few months had refused to show me anything optimistic about myself. I grabbed my hair and pulled it behind my head, tight.

Frank.

I turned sideways and examined my figure. What did that mean, exactly, to bind one's chest? I didn't have much to worry about yet, but, just in case, I still had an Ace bandage from the time I tripped in a gopher hole and sprained my ankle.

I stared at myself and in my mind walked down Frank's road again. First, he'd run away from home. He'd catch a Greyhound bus at the depot over in Willamette Junction and head on down to Florida, where the pro leagues had their spring-training camps. He'd get a job. Pumping gas. Frank Cullers would be just this blond kid down at the Shell, some kid who always smelled like gasoline, a smell so strong that when he stood out there swinging for the Local Legends the spectators swore they saw fumes rise, that when the ball exploded off his bat there were sparks and someday Frank Cullers would ignite. The scouts would be using up all their long-distance minutes jabbering to major-league management: "C'mon down and see for yourself—this kid's *blazing!*"

I dropped my hair and floated upstairs to my bedroom. I felt so good, I grabbed the McGwire Ball and rubbed it on my head for extra good luck. Then I spread my arms and grinned at my posters. "Here I come!"

The plan had to be perfect. Everything had to be coordinated smoothly. I grabbed a notebook and flopped down on my bed. "Money," I wrote. How much? I traced the word over and over in blue ink until it was dark and heavy. Money.

I wouldn't let poverty stop me. I thought of Dad's wallet, then I thought of the big checks Aunt Beth got in the mail from Torchlight Collections. No . . . I needed to steal from someone I hated, like Coach Foster. I'd watch him closely, and maybe one day soon he'd leave his wallet on the bench, or maybe on the dashboard of his car. I'd just grab it and run. It was such a malicious idea, only an anti-champ could think it up. I thought it up for Frank.

"Hack off hair" was the next thing I wrote down.

Dark sunglasses

Boy's jeans

Boy's T-shirts

Boy's jacket

Boy's sweatshirt

Boy's Nikes

Boy's hat

Ace bandage

Really big backpack

Come to think of it, I already had a lot of boy's clothes, but I wanted to look authentic, so I wrote, "Get ratty string bracelet like Steven's."

I jumped off the bed and booted up my computer. Good. Bus routes, schedules, ticket prices—all on the Internet. I printed out the times the Greyhound departed Willamette Junction for Miami. I could slip away in the early morning, on the 3:45 a.m. bus, or, if I had to grab Foster's wallet and flee, I could hide out and grab a bus at 3:25 or 9:35 p.m.

I felt like I did before a game starts: concentrated, intense. I . . . Frank . . . was going to get to play ball. Frank wouldn't be in the bush leagues for long. Those scouts would find him. If he wanted them to. But maybe he didn't want them to, maybe he wanted a life like Slow's, a hobo's life, happy, free.

Still . . . someday, some hot, humid day on some second-rate field that some small-town parks department couldn't even afford to weed, as Frank shuffled toward the plate, wouldn't someone recognize him? Someday he'd pitch against the Topanga Tremors. Something about the pitcher with the short blond hair would seem familiar to the Tremors' coach. Slow would keep his eye on the boy, watch him buzz around the infield, watch him bat, and he'd notice Frank tugging on his batting gloves just like a girl he used to know.

Of course, Frank wouldn't notice the Tremors' coach watching him. By that time, Frank would have met so many great players, had so many fun times of his own, he'd have forgotten all about his childhood friend. So, when Frank saw the Tremors' coach calling time out, striding across the infield, he'd wonder, Who's that old guy?

Then Frank would remember. His heart would feel like a ball ricocheting off the backstop. Like I felt now, just thinking about it.

Slow'd walk up. He'd reach out and tickle Frank's chin. "Soft as a baby's behind," he'd murmur, staring into my . . . Frank's eyes. "No nicks, no cuts, no five-o'clock shadow. Franny—get your butt on home. We only want champs in this game."

My heart kept ricocheting off that backstop. That's not how I wanted it to end.

Maybe he wouldn't say that. Maybe Slow would be so happy to see me again he'd arrange for a trade and I'd join the Topanga Tremors. He'd keep my secret. And then wouldn't it be really perfect? Me and Slow, together, warming the front seat of the team bus, sipping cocoa in some podunk café, chewing over last night's game. Slow'd flirt with the waitress; I'd skip over to the drugstore and buy another decal to paper the Ford.

One day we'd even play in Highwater, me and Slow in the dugout giggling over the situation. Maybe. Maybe Steven Chauppette would be in the stands. Yeah. He'd be one of those guys who used to play college ball, then had a shot at the big time but gave it up to be a math teacher or something, something responsible and dull, but every time he watched a game, his throat was so dry with regret he could barely swallow his Cracker Jacks.

Frank would hit one deep—right over the fence. Steven would turn to his friend Billy (bald and about three hundred pounds of solid beer gut by then) and say, "Remember that blond girl who hit like that?" Steven would look sad. He'd be sad a lot now that he was old. Sad, sad, sad. "I sort of miss her. I'm sorry I was so mean to her."

Perfect.

Everything was going to be perfect.

chapter 7

Aluminum bats clanked against catcher's masks and batting helmets as Coach Foster dragged an equipment bag across the bumpy field. He wore the same T-shirt practically every day: "Save a Logger. Eat a Spotted Owl."

Sipping a Slurpee, Billy slouched toward the dugout, a long arm draped around MacKenzie's neck. Mozzie and Angel pedaled in from Bryant Avenue.

Steven wouldn't look at me, so, fine, I wouldn't look at him, either. Instead I ran through my plan. In the two days since I'd thought Frank up, I'd managed to pull the entire scheme together, but a bus ticket to

Florida still cost $175, about $152.50 more than I had saved in my drawer. So I watched Foster carefully. His wallet was in his back pocket, I could tell by the bulge.

The rest of the team straggled in for practice. A car door slammed and tiny Blast barreled across the grass; he was wearing a strange headdress with a long flap hanging down over his neck, the sides pulled back and wound around the crown of his head. It looked like something a desert sheikh would wear, but it wasn't white, it was made of black shiny material. Foster noticed it right away. "What's that you're wearing?" he demanded.

"It's my do-rag," Blast said proudly.

"Well, it's disgusting. Take it off."

"It's for the sun," Blast protested.

"White people don't wear those. Take it off."

Reluctantly, Blast pulled the do-rag off his head. It wasn't for the sun—it was to hide the results of the recent blaze that had swept across his scalp. I counted seven gauze pads taped between five remaining patches of scorched hair. Obviously, Blast had found something more exciting to blow up than Molotov cocktails. Quoc started to laugh, but the crazy-mad look in Blast's eyes stopped him. It stopped everyone.

"Where's your cap?" Foster asked.

"Ashes."

"So just use a batting helmet." Foster shook his head and sighed. "Okay, okay." He waved us closer around him. "Today we're going to work on a little problem I've noticed with you guys. Most of you are pulling back from pitches. Some, just a little." He pointed at George, Hootie, and . . . me! "Some a lot." He pointed at Quoc.

I seethed. I never pulled back from pitches! How could he say that? I took a deep breath and tried to cool down. He was just trying to rattle me, again. He just said that because I was a girl.

Foster continued to explain that the ball wouldn't hurt us. "Or, if it does, it only hurts for a minute. Besides, you automatically get first base." He stopped and rummaged around in the equipment bag. "You kids know what this is?" It was a tee-ball Sof-Dot RIF, a Reduced Injury Factor ball, Level 1. We'd used Level 1 in Tiny Tots, when I was six years old. "It's softer than a regulation ball," Foster said, "so it won't hurt when it hits you. Not that much, anyway. That's our drill today: try and stand your ground while I hit you with a bad pitch. Mozzie—let's show 'em how it's done. Steven, you catch today. Everyone else fan out."

As we ran out onto the field, I watched how Angel moved. Frank would run like that. I tried to copy

Angel's loping stride, the way he leaned forward and led with his shoulders.

Mozzie shambled up to the plate and swung the bat up to his shoulder. Foster had picked him because he was slow. Now the coach aimed directly at Mozzie's waist; with a sullen look Mozzie watched the pitch hit him.

"Perfect!" Foster turned and beamed at us. "Did you guys see that? Didn't even twitch. We have a man on base now!"

"That DID hurt!" Mozzie whined.

"Looking good, Moz!" MacKenzie called. Mozzie shrugged and shuffled onto the field.

"Good job!" Foster beamed. "Okay—you." He did not even try to pronounce Quoc's name.

"It's Quack!" Billy shouted as Quoc picked up the bat.

"Quack quack quack!" Blast squawked. George made a gobbling sound. Quoc just grinned. He ducked under the coach's pitch but popped back up, smiling.

"Nice escape, Quack," Billy called. "You were almost dinner!"

Quoc jerked away from another ball. "I guess you don't understand English," Foster jeered. "Go." He pointed to the outfield. "GO!"

Quoc handed the bat to Steven and trotted out to the field. As he ran past me I heard him mumbling, "Jerk."

Now Billy swaggered up to the plate. His tongue lolled out of his mouth in a cocky grin. Even his nose smirked.

"Give it to me right here, Coach," he called, pointing to his left arm. He stepped into the first pitch and let it roll off his shoulder. Laughing, he turned and high-fived Steven. I noticed that Steven didn't smile.

"That's my man," Foster called. "Do it again. Show these girls how it's done."

It should have been obvious to everybody that Foster was easing up on his pitches for Billy. Billy stepped into another pitch, and then, for good measure and extra bragging rights, a third. After that, with some encouragement, George and then Angel stood their ground and let the coach draw a bead on them.

"HOOTIE?" Foster roared. "Let's see what you're made of, son."

Hootie Foster slunk across the field. Steven handed him the bat, and Hootie carefully inspected the handle. He pointed at something, and Steven handed him another bat, which Hootie also checked for faults. But he couldn't dilly-dally forever.

"Batter up!" his father called impatiently.

Hootie wiped his sweating palms on his shorts and stepped into the box, but when the pitch came at him, he lost his nerve and swung. The bat slipped from his grasp—and sailed toward the pitcher's mound.

"HEY!" Foster screamed as the bat spun by his left ear.

I collapsed on the grass, I was laughing so hard.

"Did you do that on PURPOSE, you little punk?" Foster yelled, running toward the plate.

"Coach!" Steven cried. The coach stumbled to a halt and, glaring at Hootie, wiped the spit from his mouth with the back of his hand. Hootie walked backwards until he bumped into the backstop. The field was deathly quiet. I wasn't laughing anymore.

"Okay, Francine Cullers!" Foster yelled. He whirled and marched back toward the pitcher's mound. "Now it's *your* turn to torture me!"

I practiced Frank's run across the infield. When I pretended I was Frank, I felt better. Soon this gang of losers would be three thousand miles behind me, and I could be Frank forever.

"I don't pull back," I informed Foster. "Not even 'a little.'"

"Yes you do."

What a . . . Now I was *really* mad! I'd show him, though.

My favorite bat was lying by Steven's feet, but he turned his head and ignored me. Everyone had a point to make, it seemed.

"Yuck. Girl germs," Billy yelled as I took a practice swing.

"Don't wipe them off, Smythe," I answered. "Maybe you'll catch what I have and improve."

Billy got a fake coughing fit. The rest of the team caught on, and as I stepped up to the plate, the raucous coughing got louder and louder.

Mature.

But then I lost it. "SMYTHE, YOU—" Wait! Did I really see that? As the boys coughed and I started toward Billy, did Foster drop the RIF and pick a regulation ball out of the equipment bag?

Ooooomph! I jerked back and swung my bat just in time. The ball flew into right field. No RIF would have carried that far.

"Hey!"

Foster reached into the bag and plucked out another ball.

"Let me see that!" I yelled.

"Okay!" He hurled it straight at me. I gasped,

jumped back, and swung. CRACK! Home run, I thought proudly, and then—yikes!—swung again.

"Are you trying to"—another rocket came straight at my head, but I slapped it back just in time—"*kill* me?" His eyes narrowed into slits; his top lip pulled down and curled. A monster.

"What are you afraid of, girlie?" He reached into the bag again. "Can't take the heat? Can't play with the guys?" I hammered another ball into right field. He'd brushed me back three feet from the batter's box. . . . There was no time to think, no time to scream, no time to run, because he fired, and then he fired again.

"Fran!" Steven's voice was somewhere far behind me, but nobody really existed outside of Foster.

Another missile. Another. Twenty balls? Forty? How many balls were in that bag? Still they kept coming.

My bat was my shield now. I was swinging to defend myself.

He was trying to take baseball away from me.

"Run, Fran!"

Let him nail me—*crack*—let him knock me cold—*crack*—give it to me—*crack*—give it again—*crack*—I wouldn't run!

YOU CAN'T TAKE THIS—*crack*—AWAY FROM ME!

78

Steven was screaming, "Stop it! Stop it!"

There was nothing now except hard white rocks spinning at my head, and me swinging.

"STOP IT!"

And then I was swinging but there were no balls— I just couldn't stop.

"She's a girl, man! She's a *girl!*" Someone was screaming that. Billy Smythe.

Pain shot up my arms. My ears were ringing— everything seemed far away, unreal—but I saw Billy hanging on Coach Foster's back, arms wrapped around his neck, screaming in his ear. And wrapped around Foster's arm, weighting it down, was Steven.

Like claws, Foster's fingers opened and closed around one last ball. I stared. He stared. I panted. He panted.

"Help us, guys!" Billy yelled. Blast streaked across the infield and pried the ball out of Foster's hand. Angel and George ran in, too, and grabbed Foster's other arm. The Hardwares were crawling all over Foster, but he barely noticed them. The infield lights popped on. Still he stared at me.

Then Mozzie was running in from the parking lot, and a string of parents, I don't even know how many, were running behind him. A big man in a checkered shirt shouted, "What's going on here?" and Billy told him all about it.

"Give me the bat, Franny." It was Steven, still far away. I was afraid to take my eyes off Foster. "C'mon, Franny, it's over. Give me the bat."

It weighed fifty tons. I wondered how Steven could possibly lift it off my shoulder, but he reached out and plucked it out of my hands. Just like that.

Wheezing, I looked around. MacKenzie had her fingers pressed to her lips. Quoc was squeezing his face. Hootie's lips were pulled tight over his teeth, and tears slipped down his cheeks.

"Good job," Steven said. He wouldn't come into focus, and I could barely hear him over the roaring sound in my ears. I saw him reach out like he was going to high-five me, but then he stopped pretending it was okay, and I felt his arm around my shoulders. "You did great."

I started shaking in the cool evening air.

The man in the checkered shirt was pulling Foster off the mound, but Foster whirled and pointed a finger at me.

He shouted, "Hey, girlie. You know what? You're what's wrong. Not me. *You.*"

I couldn't stop shaking.

"You and everyone like you, you're what's wrong with . . . with *everything.*"

chapter 8

I ran up the driveway, through the cool shadows on the back lawn; I ran across the back porch and burst into the kitchen. There was a single light on over the sink. A rooster-shaped salt shaker crowed silently atop Aunt Beth's note: "Franny—gone shopping. Be back as soon as the checks starts bouncing. You know where the cookies are."

The only sounds in the house were the tick of the clock on the stove, the tap of my rubber cleats across the linoleum, and the tornado of my heart pounding against my ribs. I fell into a chair and tried to ease my shuddering breaths. Safe at last. And yet . . . not safe. Out of the corner of my eye, Foster's missiles kept belting me. I wrapped my arms around my head and pressed my forehead to the table. What would Frank have done? But Foster wouldn't have attacked Frank. There was nothing wrong with Frank. Florida, Florida, Florida. I knocked my head against the table. I'd be safe there.

The phone rang in the studio. I squeezed my eyes shut and counted the rings until the message machine picked up. "Hi! This is Cullers' Illustration. . . ." Aunt Beth's cheerful voice floated down the hall.

There was a beep, then Mrs. Chauppette's voice spoke urgently. "J.J., you need to call me. Something happened tonight. Call me as soon as you get in, okay?" Then the machine clicked off, and the only sound was the loud ticking of that stupid clock.

Mrs. Chauppette. Always trying to act like my mother.

I pressed my forehead harder into the table and held my head tighter. Stupid jock strap! I yanked it out of my hair, catapulted myself across the kitchen, and snatched scissors out of a drawer. After I'd sliced the jock strap into a million billion little shreds, I pushed it to the bottom of the trash. Only one thing could make me feel better than that did. Bed.

Someone was sitting in the living room. I didn't think my heart could ride any lower in my chest tonight, but now it slammed down to my knees. "Dad?" I whispered. I'd thought he was finished with sitting in the dark alone.

After a few seconds, he stirred. "Yeah," he said. "Right here."

"Are you okay?"

In answer, he reached out his hand. I saw the solid shape lift against the light of the window. I took his hand, but I wasn't sure what I should do, so I just stood there, holding it lightly. It was cold. I couldn't see his face, and that was probably okay by him, because he reached up with his other hand and wiped his cheeks. Neither of us turned on the light. I didn't want him to see my face, either.

He held something in his lap. "What's that, Dad?"

"Oh. An old scarf. I found it under the back seat of the car. Weird, that I'd never cleaned under the back seat before, but today I thought, Well, time to clean this old junker up. Get some things done. New lease on life and all that."

I couldn't really see it in the dark, but I knew it was a scarf that had belonged to Mom.

He took his hand back and rubbed his palms along his knees. "How was your game?"

I sat down on the couch and stared at his silhouette against the window. Suddenly I missed his Pretend

Dad voice, because this voice was too sad. "It was just practice," I said.

"Ah." I saw his head turn to profile as he gazed back over his shoulder, outside. "I used to love practice when I was your age. Running those drills. Hard, but after you're done, everything seems right with the world."

"Well, this was different." But right now my problems didn't seem as big as his, so I just said, "He's picking on me, Dad."

"Who?"

"Coach Foster."

Dad nodded. "Coaches are tough sometimes, Franny. Sometimes they're not fair, sometimes they're downright bastards. 'It's all about the team,' though, that's what Slow says, so just keep that in mind. You're a tough kid. I know you can handle it."

"But . . ." I wanted to say more, but all of a sudden he pressed the scarf against his forehead. He held it there a long time, while the crickets out on the lawn pulsed. Finally, he handed it to me.

"Would you put this in the closet upstairs?" he asked.

"Sure." I stood up. I'm tough, I thought. I can handle this.

"What did Mrs. Chauppette want?"

I stared down at the scarf. "Something about a bake sale, I think." Bake sale. Who would buy that? Dad would. "I'll tell Aunt Beth to call her, okay?"

"Okay." As I left, I heard the TV flicker on, then the happy chatter of some summer rerun. I walked down the hall and into the studio. There were two messages on the machine. The other was from Slow; he wanted Dad to call him, was checking up on him after their conversation. Probably about me. I pressed rewind and erased both messages. Then I slowly walked up the stairs to the second-floor closet Aunt Beth gave us to store our extra things. In it was a box we'd packed with some of Mom's clothes, the things that reminded us of her, the ones we couldn't bear to donate to the Goodwill. A dress she'd worn to her best friend's wedding. A sweater she'd loved. I folded the scarf and put it on top of the sweater. I put my nose down in the box, but her smell wasn't there anymore. I'd lost that, too.

I cried in big, hiccuping gulps but swallowed them, so Dad wouldn't hear.

Then I walked upstairs to the third floor. Cullers' Classic All Stars were in my bedroom. They broke out of their huddle and looked at me grimly. Casey went and stared out the window. Willie Mays touched my shoulder. Jackie Robinson just kept shaking his head.

They watched me as I kicked off my shoes and scrunched down to the bottom of the bed, pulled the covers up, and tried to stop shaking.

"It's okay," Lou Gehrig said softly.

No, it's not.

"Yes, it is," Jackie said. "You're tough."

chapter 9

It wasn't me who was taking the money.

It was Frank.

It was Frank who crept barefooted down the stairs, who found Aunt Beth's backpack on the second-floor landing, who coaxed the zipper open.

"Help me, save me! Help me! Save me!" Aunt Beth was fooling around in the studio downstairs, psyching herself up for work. Her voice rose through the new gas-heating system. "Saaaaave me!" she squeaked. There was a low rumbling, then the names "Torchlight Collections" and "Mary Read" knocked against the aluminum ducts.

Frank peeked inside the backpack. Aunt Beth's

address book, keys, hairbrush—wallet. It was of very old leather, with pansies stitched along the front, a wallet that Aunt Beth had found at an antique store. "It's at least a hundred years old," she'd told me. "Think of all the money that's passed through there— a million bucks, maybe. Makes me feel rich."

A million bucks! If only it was all still there. Aunt Beth wouldn't notice a few hundred thousand gone. It was strange, handling the wallet without permission. It felt slippery, cool.

A chill ran up my fingers. I gulped—no, I couldn't.

But Frank could. He wanted to get to Florida and he knew what he had to do. He flicked the old-fashioned brass latch and looked inside.

Seven lousy bucks. Some loose change.

I tried to feel like Frank some more, but I couldn't. Seven dollars! It was such a small amount that if I were to take even a dollar Aunt Beth would notice. I hesitated. Florida, I thought, everything will be all right in Florida. So I took a dollar anyway. Just to get into the practice. Just to get used to how it felt to be a big old champless thief.

It felt bad, even if I was planning to pay her back. Everything felt bad. My throat scratched and my bones ached. My eyes were swollen. As I closed the wallet and put it in the backpack again and arranged everything so that it wouldn't look suspicious, I thought about all the nice things I'd buy for Aunt Beth someday. I folded the dollar up about twenty times and stuck it in the tiny coin pocket in my waistband. For practice.

"Franny!" I jumped. Aunt Beth had her mouth up close to the grate in the first-floor hallway. "A prince to seeee yooooou, Rapunzel," she trilled.

I tiptoed down to the first-floor landing. . . . Prince indeed. Steven stood in the front hallway, scratching a mosquito bite.

"I told you that guy was going to snap!" he shouted when he saw me peeking around the corner.

"Shhhhh!" I hoped Aunt Beth hadn't heard. "C'mere—" I motioned him upstairs.

"You didn't tell your aunt?" he said incredulously. There weren't any radiators close by, but I glared at Steven and held my finger to my lips until he promised to whisper.

"It doesn't matter," I said. "Aunt Beth has a lot to worry about right now. Like my dad—I think he's sad again."

That shut him up. I had never told him much, but he seemed to know how bad it had been over the winter. For a minute I imagined the conversation around the Chauppette dinner table. Mrs. Chauppette would say things like, "You be nice to that little girl, her mom is dead and her dad had a mental breakdown," and "Your dad and I may be divorced, Steven, but at least we're all still sane."

"Please don't tell." I had to convince him. "I—I want to talk to them myself, and I'll know when the time is right. Later today or tomorrow." Besides, I thought, where I'm going, I'm never going to have to think about that homicidal coach or that flea-bitten, ragtag bunch of quote-unquote teammates ever again. But I didn't say that.

Still, his eyes narrowed in suspicion. "Foster's been suspended."

"What?"

"You don't have to worry about him anymore. The parks department is going to find us another coach. You can come back to the team."

Like that was supposed to be a relief. I imagined the scene—Coach Foster pulled out of a cop car, the perp walk through the parks-department parking lot, the accusations, the trial, the lawyers, the man in the checkered shirt with his hand on a Bible—and for the first time in twelve hours I felt a little better. "Then there's no reason to worry my aunt or my dad about this, right?"

His mouth was puckered up in that Saint Steven look. "Right?" I prodded.

He relaxed. "Okay."

Things were a little awkward then. One, I think we both realized that until recently we hadn't been speaking. Two, I wanted to thank Steven for helping me last night, but, then again, I didn't want to talk about it anymore. Three, I was in my pajamas. Four, my hair was sticking straight out from my head. Five, my eyes were all swollen. So, when Steven suggested we ride over to Willamette Stadium and watch the university game, or go hit some balls, or something, anything, it was a relief to dash to my room and pull a Seattle Mariners jersey over my head. Outside, the trees swayed and a breeze sighed through the room, rustling the Classic All Stars.

"Where's your bike?" Steven was on the front porch with my Adidas bag slung over his shoulder. I realized that I'd left my bike at the field last night.

"Gotcha," he said. "Billy is keeping it for you."

So we had to ride his bike, both of us together; we'd done it a lot when we were kids, but it'd been a long time since we practiced. I hoisted the Adidas bag onto my back, then tightened the strap across my chest. It was so heavy I felt like I was going to tip backwards. I sat on the seat; Steven had to stand straight up on the pedals and use his full weight to get the bike moving. We only fell over once.

We took the pedestrian path over the highway. I thought glumly of Billy spitting on my bicycle seat as we rattled across the footbridge over the Willamette River and turned up Elm Street. Clinton Hill was too steep for Steven to pedal up with two people and a sack, so he pushed the bike and I lugged the bag. We cut through our old neighborhood. From the top of the hill the university field spread out below us. We hopped back on and coasted downhill; I held tight to Steven's waist, but all of a sudden, for the first time ever, I felt embarrassed, so I grabbed his belt instead.

"Nice bracelet."

"Don't start."

The Junction Javas moved around the field like big-league hopefuls. It was only a practice game, but the bleachers were filled with friends and family.

"Those guys are scouts." I pointed them out to Steven, two tired-looking men, spotted with mustard and coffee stains, sitting as far apart from each other as the benches allowed. One stared off into the parking lot; the other rummaged through his potato chips. Every once in a while, their eyes would sneak back to the players.

"Nah. How do you know?"

"I see them around at all levels of games."

"Maybe they'll scout us." Steven grinned. We were loosening up now, shaking off the awkwardness, getting back to the way we'd always felt around each other. We found a stretch of field where we could keep an eye on the Javas but still have room to run our own practice. A Styrofoam cup served as home plate, and a stray candy-bar wrapper as the pitching rubber. I threw some balls to Steven, and pretty soon we were in the middle of our own imaginary commentary.

"Top of the third," I said, going into a slo-mo windup. "Record crowds here at Yankee Stadium—"

"Shea Stadium," Steven said, frowning. His dad had grown up in Queens, so Steven was one of those pathetic Mets fans who just couldn't accept reality.

"—here at Yankee Stadium." They're winners, why fight it? "Cullers has just relieved Clemens. Steven Chauppette is struggling, folks. He still hasn't got the sense to open his stance like his friend Fran keeps telling him. . . ." Steven rearranged his feet. I fired the ball over the Styrofoam cup, and he caught it square in the middle. "I told you!" I ran after the ball, making the fake cheering noise that always annoys Aunt Beth. When I turned, Steven was facing the distant scouts, bowing.

"Now it's Chauppette's turn to put away Cussed Cullers, folks," Steven announced. We traded places and I banged the bat on the cup. Crouching low, I waggled the tip high over my head. He coiled into his windup. "Go, Chauppette! Booooo, Cullers!" He pitched.

The ball hurtled—straight at me—

Steven stared, wide-eyed.

"What happened?"

"I don't know." I ran down the ball, which was dribbling through the grass behind me. "Nothing. . . . Pitch me another."

But I did know. It was like last night.

Steven looked worried. "I've never seen you do that before."

"All right, all right. Just throw me another one."

Steven pitched again.

"Fran! You didn't even swing! You just . . ." There was heat in Steven's eyes. "That bastard! What did he do to you?"

I turned and ran after that ball, too. Ten seconds ago, I'd seen it spinning toward me, and—

I'd bailed. I'd lost my guts.

After a minute, Steven suggested we try again. "Wipe your mind of yesterday," he said. "You're a pro. You can only think about the game, nothing else is allowed. You have absolutely no right to think about anything else—not even the feel of the sun on your face—nothing but the ball that is coming at you right now!" The pitch came at me, soft and easy. I concentrated, real hard. I wiped my mind of everything.

The ball came at me and—

It was bad. So bad it had a name: The Flinch.

"See what I mean?" Steven said. "You were thinking about what I was saying! You should have just been waiting for the ball."

"I think I need a lighter bat," I bluffed. "This one's really heavy." But it was *my* bat. I'd been using it all season.

Steven walked slowly toward me. "Here, let me look at your grip." I swung the bat in slow motion as he studied my hands. Nothing was different. My grip wasn't the problem.

He caught the end of my bat and guided it gently through the air, like you do for a little kid. "How's that feel?"

"Like someone's holding the end of my bat."

"Smartass." He turned and stomped back to the candy-bar wrapper.

"Steven. No more."

"C'mon, Fran, I know you. This is just a hitch.

We'll work through it. Ten minutes, we'll have it licked."

But it wasn't a hitch. It wasn't even a slump. This thing was dark; it was sticky. I'd been running from this feeling since the day Mom died, and now it had its bony hands wound around my neck. I knew I would never escape. Florida, Frank, the minors, playing with Slow on the Topanga Tremors—it was all over.

I'd set out to destroy the Hardwares—but they had destroyed me.

chapter 10

Here's what happens when a player goes into a slump:
it's all he can think about. It's a rock in the road
blocking his way, so he works real hard at getting
around it. Practices, practices day and night. Hires
special coaches. Or starts seeing a shrink. That doesn't
work, so he consults witch doctors, healers, medicine
men. Throughout, he keeps practicing. And the more
he practices, the more he practices the very thing
that's wrong. His mind is screaming *"No!"* but his
body has seized the slump.

Or—the slump has seized him.

I knew all the stories. One day, Steve Blass went
wild, and he could never throw a decent pitch again.

He looked fine in warm-up, but as soon as the game started, he bounced pitches, he hit batters, he threw behind them. . . . They call it Steve Blass disease, because other great pitchers have caught it. The catcher Mackey Sasser forgot how to throw the ball to the pitcher. Chuck Knoblauch developed a mental block and couldn't throw to first base from second, but he was lucky. All those other guys were dumped, but the Yankees stuck Knoblauch in the outfield. No one would ever give me a second chance, because they wouldn't give me a first chance. I'd never make it out of Junior League.

The Flinch meant The End.

I stood in the middle of my room and gazed around me. The Camp Carmichael brochures, the signed photos of the Yankees, the snapshots of the Rosewood Baggers and the Topanga Tremors, the pictures of Dad and Slow on the Applegate A's, the series pennants, my fifty-two "Greatest Games" self-made VHS tapes plus a VHS *Life and Times* collection, the postcards from Slow, the New York Yankees wooden wall clock, my Bobble Head collection, my Little League Golden Gloves trophies, the ball-shaped Yankee air freshener, the Reggie Jackson plate, the Yankees–versus–Red Sox chess set, the Mike Piazza action figure, the 1965 Mets Old-Timers Day program (near-mint), the beautiful Bill Goff Vintage National and American League Ballparks posters, the "Cubs Suck!" and "Mets Are Pond Scum!" pins stuck up on my curtains, even the Yankees 2000 World Series lightswitch cover . . . all that and more needed to fit into the three big boxes I'd hauled up from the basement.

A couple of hours into it, Aunt Beth called me down to dinner. "I'm busy!"

"Too busy for pizza?"

Too busy. There were patches of dust all over my empty shelves that had to be wiped clean. I scraped the Yankees decals off the window with a razor blade, then I searched the house for a new duvet cover, since the one I was using was approved by the National League. Even my bottom sheet had to go: it was blue pinstripes. A stack of dusty old *Sports Illustrated* magazines was practically holding up my bed; I strapped duct tape around those and carried them down to the recycling spot at the side of the house. On my way back upstairs I found Aunt Beth's pack and paid her back her dollar. I didn't need it anymore. Behind the magazines was a bunch of broken equipment I'd pushed back there—I hauled it all downstairs to the trash.

I pulled the Mariners jersey off.

I didn't let myself think about what I was doing.

I just worked on autopilot. Every time a question rose in my mind, I swatted it down. Every time a sad spot blossomed on my heart, I squashed it with one thought: The Flinch.

"What are you doing up there, Franny?" Aunt Beth called.

"Cleaning my room."

She didn't have an answer, that's how shocked she was. I heard a soft "Wow!" drift through the heating ducts.

After a few hours, almost everything was packed. I wrestled the boxes down the stairs to the storage area on the second-floor landing, the closet where we'd put Mom's stuff. The closet was so deep Aunt Beth had considered making it into a third bathroom, so there was plenty of room for extra boxes. They scraped reluctantly over the rough floorboards when I pushed them back. Then I pulled the Yankees beanbag chair down the stairs and pushed it in there, too.

Maybe, just maybe, now that my nose wasn't all stuffed with crying, I could smell a little bit of Mom's perfume lingering in the box we'd packed her clothes in. I lifted the lid and breathed deep. The tiniest whiff was still there.

Only a few things were left in my room; the things that meant the most to me. Like the McGwire Ball. It couldn't help me anymore, but Dad still needed it, even if he didn't realize it. He wasn't home from work yet, so I went downstairs and looked into his room. Where could I hide it? Under the bed—I bent down and pushed it far back against the wall, by the bed leg, then scooped some dust bunnies up around it for camouflage. I wanted to roll it across my head once more, just for old times' sake. I stopped myself. That ritual was for good luck, but there was no power strong enough to fight The Flinch.

I was standing on top of my dresser prying the last thumbtack off the wall when I looked through the window and saw Steven roll into the backyard. He was riding his bike, balancing mine beside him. I heard a knock, then Steven came clomping up the stairs. He stood in my doorway and stared.

"I don't like this," he said. "I don't like this at all."

I let go of the last poster, Jackie Robinson, and let it drift down to the bed, where it settled on the other Classic All Stars. I looked around. The blank walls, pocked by thumbtack holes, glared a naked white. My bookshelves were empty except for a set of Aunt Beth's old encyclopedias that had been there when I moved in. I hopped down and gathered the posters, rolled them together, and looped a rubber band around the whole bunch.

"Don't you think you're being a bit overdramatic?" Steven asked.

"Nope." Is a wake overdramatic? I thought. The coffin, the flowers, the black clothes—it's a ceremony to mark what's gone, and this was my career's funeral.

That gave me an idea. After I put the posters in the second-floor closet, I trotted back upstairs. Steven was sitting gingerly on the edge of the bed, looking around uneasily.

"Why are you wearing a skirt?" he asked.

"Everything else had baseball logos on it. I'm lucky I had this one T-shirt from the Gap."

He shook his head in exasperation. "I really think you're going too far. We'll get to it bright and early tomorrow, Fran. I know we can work this problem out."

"I'm quitting, Steven."

"What?"

"Look around you. I quit."

His face scrunched up so I couldn't tell if he was going to laugh or yell. "Don't be such a girl."

But those insults couldn't hurt me now. They had made the old Fran mad, the Fran that was going to be a baseball pro someday, and I was going to learn to live without her. There was just one thing left to do. I opened my desk drawer (three pencils with baseball-shaped erasers, I'd missed those) and fished out the Greyhound bus schedule I'd printed off the Internet.

I knew that Steven would follow, so I headed out to the yard.

"Thanks for bringing my bike."

"Where are we going now?" he asked, pedaling after me.

"Over to Willamette Junction again. Shhhhh . . ." Be quiet now, I thought, because I need to imagine them one more time: Cullers' Classic All Stars had followed us down the stairs and across the back lawn; Steven couldn't see them, but in the cool summer evening they loped along beside us. Maris and Gehrig were laughing, tossing a ball back and forth over the street as they ran; Rose, Koufax, and Johnny Bench jogged easily, chatting amongst themselves; only Jackie looked worried.

Frank was there, too.

Me and Steven and fifteen All Time Greats pulled up outside the Willamette Greyhound station.

"What are we doing here?" Steven asked.

"I just need to see something."

The station didn't look like the doorway to a new future. It looked like a cattle shed with vending machines. The concrete floor inside was grimy with diesel dust and spotted with black patches of flattened gum. There were about eight people standing around, and every single one looked beaten down. I noticed a man with his foot up on a box strapped with tape, and I wondered what dreams he'd sealed up in there. On either side of me the building stretched away, long and narrow; it was just a few short steps to another pair of doors opposite; outside, I could see the empty yard.

Steven scooted straight over to the glowing soda machine and fished around in the coin pocket for stray change. Then he checked the telephone. It was a habit he'd picked up during his parents' divorce, when his mom was working three jobs.

The ticket window was closed, but the Babe rapped on the steel grate and, just like I knew it would, the window rolled open. An old man stuck his cigar behind his ear and pulled out the cash box. I watched the All Stars standing in line. Casey Stengel fished his wallet out of his back pocket and pushed some bills across the counter. He paid for himself and Frank. The rest waited in line with crossed arms, jostling and laughing, running old stories back and forth as they waited.

Steven watched me quizzically, then drifted toward a sheet of Plexiglas mounted on the far wall; a crooked line of posters was trapped under it: runaways. His worried look zipped back and forth between me and the posters.

Finally, the last All Star had his ticket. Willie Mays stood at the door waving the other players through, patting one on the back, taking a playful jab at another. He straightened his face and took a mock bow when I passed through. Outside, it was dark. Through the distant wire fence I could see stars and the bulky shapes of parked buses. The wind blew across the yard, scooping grit and wrappers and one lone soda can.

"Are we meeting someone?" Steven asked. "Is Slow coming in?" He was turning this trip around and around in his head, trying to figure it out.

"Just a few minutes more, Steven. Then we can go home, I promise."

The man with the box shuffled out the door. Others soon joined him. I looked at my watch: 9:32.

Then I saw it, riding against the darkening sky, the silhouette of the 9:35 to Florida. Its headlights swept the yard; its back wheels missed the driveway and lumbered up over the curb. The customers stepped forward, and the All Stars grew quiet. They were sleepy now; it'd been a long, emotional day. Gehrig yawned, and that started off the whole bunch yawning and stretching. As the silver-paneled bus parked and the driver stepped down, Ruth touched me on my shoulder, chucked me under the chin. Mays did, too, and then, as the driver tossed their bags into the baggage compartment, the others were surrounding me, patting my head, slapping my neck, rubbing my shoulders; Roberto Clemente even squeezed my nose, and I thought I saw tears in his eyes.

Come with us.

It will be great.

We need you. . . .

But I shook my head; the driver called "All aboard!" and I stood my ground as Cullers' Classic All Stars filed onto the bus. The ceiling lights inside haloed the tops of their heads. They took seats along one side and pressed their hands to the windows, staring down at me.

Frank was the last aboard. He stepped forward, and I saw that we were almost identical: same height, same blond hair, same dreams. He jerked his chin at the bus: C'mon.

No. Go with them.

You're the boss.

He was shaking his head, but he climbed the steps. The driver grabbed the long handle and drew the door closed. The airbrake gasped as it was released, and the bus trundled down Main Street. I watched its taillight blinking yellow at the corner stop sign; then it turned and headed south, toward Florida.

I squeezed my arms into my chest, watching it go. Even with Steven staring at me, I couldn't help it, I uncrossed my arms—I waved.

"What are you doing, Fran?"

Saying good-bye to some old friends.

chapter 11

Living without baseball was like learning to live without Mom all over again.

The rain had set in the night before she died. Mom had an early-morning meeting. "Bye, Fran!" she called, but I didn't know it'd be forever. I heard her car back out of the drive, then the sound of the rain dripping off the rhododendrons outside my window. An hour later, I was printing my homework assignment when a red light started flashing around my room. I looked out the window and there was a police car in the driveway; I walked down the hallway and Dad was sitting against the open front door, his hands pressed into his eyes. The rain came slanting into the hallway. There was a policeman, a young guy, with tears clumping his eyelashes. That's when I knew.

"Oh, honey," the policeman said.

Later, Aunt Beth told me that some man who'd been drinking too much had run a stop sign at ninety miles per hour.

I had to unlearn everything about life up until twelve years. Little things, like who makes breakfast (not Mom, me). Who helps me shop for school supplies (not Mom, the lady at the drugstore). Who rubs my head so I can go to sleep at night (not Mom, me using the McGwire Ball). I had to find a new way to do everything, and then do it the new way over and over until I got it right.

Practice, practice, practice.

But while I was practicing, there were so many things that reminded me of her. I'd hear the water turn on upstairs, and I'd think she was washing her hair. Until I remembered. I'd hear keys jangling in the hallway, and I'd think it was Mom coming home. I'd find her bobby pins behind the sofa cushion and think, Mom needs these. And every time I remembered, I'd go outside and drag the equipment bag out from under her old lawn chair and I'd throw one hundred pitches against the side of the house.

It was the Big Sad. I had to call Aunt Beth every

morning so that she could drive over and make Dad get out of bed and go to work. She brought cereal and made him eat it in front of her, just to be sure he really ate. When I'd call her because he was sitting in the dark and it scared me, she'd drive over again and turn on all the lights. Finally, she moved us into her house in South Highwater, so that she could "keep an eye on things."

So, while I was learning to live without Mom, I was also learning to live without Dad. Who coached the Rosewood Baggers? Not Dad, another kid's father. Who drove me to practice, who hollered my name when I made a good play? Not Dad, Mrs. Chauppette. Who practiced with me in the backyard every morning? Not Dad, Cullers' Classic All Stars. Who fought me for the McGwire Ball, who debated over the sports page? Not Dad. No one.

There were so many things that reminded me of Dad, too, but I practiced living without him. Day by day, month by month, eventually it got a little easier.

So now I knew I could learn to live without baseball.

• • •

About two days passed before Aunt Beth noticed.

She walked into the kitchen and threw the newspaper on the table. "Here," she said, unfolding it and handing me the sports section.

"Oh. No thanks."

"Really?" She peered at me over her glasses, then read the headlines. "You don't have to worry. The Yanks won."

I clapped my hands over my ears. "Don't tell me!"

"Sorry! Did I ruin the surprise? Here. . . ." She tried to hand me the page again, but I just stared down at my cereal.

"Uh, are you okay?"

"Yeah." And then, because she was still staring at me, "I'm not into all that anymore."

"Okaaaaay." Aunt Beth shuffled the sports section back into the paper. Then, without looking at me, she went to a drawer, pulled a pan out, and started to heat some milk on the stove. I ate my cereal. Since I eat it without milk, the crunching rattled my eardrums. When Aunt Beth was done, she set a steaming mug of cocoa in front of me and took her seat with her own breakfast.

"So," she said, "what *are* you into now?"

"Don't know yet."

"Baseball took up a lot of your time, didn't it? Have any other hobbies?"

"It wasn't a *hobby*."

"Oops, sorry. Of course not." She sipped her cocoa and thought. "It was a way of life, wasn't it? Sort of like . . . me being an artist, say. A calling."

I could see where she was rowing before she'd even dipped a paddle in the pond. But maybe I did need a hobby. I'd never had one.

"Would you teach me to paint, Aunt Beth?" Maybe I could be an artist, too. Maybe it ran in the family.

"Sure." She dragged it out, just like she'd dragged out "Okay," but after breakfast we left the plates on the table and Aunt Beth led me into her studio. She cleared a place on her worktable and brought me a stack of paper, a jar of water, some brushes, and a big plastic dish with little puddles of dry paint. She showed me how to wet the watercolors. She mixed blue and red together and made purple. Red and yellow made orange. It wasn't that interesting, but it made me forget how blue the sky was outside, how green the grass, how perfect a day it was for baseball.

"So," she said at last, taking a seat beside me and picking up a brush, "what should we paint first?"

I stared at the paper. I couldn't think of a thing.

Well, I thought of lots of things, really, except all of them were outlawed. I thought of a baseball—that would be easy. Just a round circle with some lines for stitching. I thought of a mitt. That would be harder.

Maybe . . . Jackie Robinson. I had to put the brush down and just stare at the paper.

Aunt Beth reached out and held my head against her shoulder. I pressed my nose into her T-shirt. "Do you want to tell me about it?" she asked, finally.

"No." I wiped my nose on the back of my hand. She handed me an oily rag.

"Are those boys being mean to you again?"

"No."

So she stopped asking me questions, and instead she showed me how to really paint. It's not about mixing colors, she said. It's about looking past what you expect to see, and seeing what's really there in front of you.

"Let's draw a flower. That's easy, right? Everyone knows a flower looks like this. . . ." She drew a circle with her brush, then she added five tooth-shaped petals, a straight line for the stem, and two triangle-shaped leaves.

I tried to copy her. Mine was a little lopsided, but it looked like a flower, too. While I was getting it right, Aunt Beth went outside and returned with a bouquet from the front yard.

"That's good!" she said. "But is that really a flower?" (I hoped so. It had been a lot of work.) "Does it look like this red rose," she asked, "which looks different from this red rose?" She used her brush to point out the flowers in the vase. "How about this blue flower?" She picked it out and laid it in front of us on the table. "It doesn't look like anything in the world but itself."

Quickly, she started to sketch the shapes that made the blue flower. She saw everything: the way some petals were smaller than the others, the way the stem was mushy from hitting the bottom of the vase, the brown edges of a tiny hole an insect had munched in one of the leaves. "The trick is to look past what you expect to see, Fran. See what's in front of you."

We spent the rest of the morning staring at the blue flower. I still couldn't understand how Aunt Beth could waste all those beautiful days indoors, just making something on a piece of paper. Nevertheless, every time my mind wandered back to the sports page on the kitchen table, every time I itched to check out the score, just this once, I'd concentrate harder.

Not thinking about baseball was really tough. But it was a matter of practice. Just like everything.

chapter 12

I'd just started to think that perhaps I did have an artist's calling when the Hardwares came to test my resolve.

"I wish I could concentrate like you can, Franny," Aunt Beth said the next morning. "That flower's dead. You can draw it while it rots, but I've got some work to finish up. Why don't you take a break? Enjoy the day and scout around for something else to paint later on."

Outside. A beautiful day. Time on my hands. It was exactly the situation I was trying to avoid. I cut through the alleyway and down the hill, straight in the other direction from the American Legion field, and pretty soon I was down by the river. Steven and I used to spend a lot of time down here skipping stones, dropping rocks in the water, aimless fun like that. Today the water was warm; it snoozed around the flat boulders while water skeeters zoomed back and forth, measuring each pool's dimensions. I poked along the bank, looking for possible still-life subjects, and found a squashed beer can and some kid's old GI Joe doll, legless and mossy. Interesting. I waded farther downstream, the current tugging at my knees.

"Hey!"

I froze. The voice came from above me. Feet scuffled through the dry grass, and a scrimmage of boys burst from the woods and galloped along the path above me. I pressed myself to the muddy underbank. I recognized Billy's swagger; Angel and Blast were with him. Their feet pounded over my head; then they were gone.

Except for Steven. "Here she is!" He peered down at me. "I knew we'd find you down here."

"Steven! Shhhhh!" He ignored the finger I held to my lips; in fact, he looked exasperated. Billy, Angel, and Blast came thundering back, and I looked for a rock to defend myself with.

"It's not like that anymore, Fran. Everyone promised," Steven said, but just then Billy looked over his shoulder and sneered. I braced myself.

"Hey," Billy said.

Hey?

Blast's head and shoulders popped up over the bank, followed by Angel's. "Hey," Angel said.

Then Blast, "Hey!" Casual. Friendly. Sincere.

I nearly slipped and drowned, I was so shocked.

"Why weren't you at practice last night?" Billy demanded. I could only stare up at him in disbelief. "We've lost Hootie, you know. We rearranged the positions, but we had to play without a shortstop. And since you didn't show up, we only had two out-fielders."

"Wait a minute. . . ." I started to explain to him that until recently I hadn't even been welcome on the Hardwares. Then I remembered that I'd given up baseball, and I let my anger just wash away. Whatever mind game Billy was playing, I didn't care anymore. "Didn't Steven tell you? I quit."

"Quit?" Billy jeered. Angel frowned. Blast just shook his head and picked at a new Band-Aid on his arm.

"Told you so," Steven said.

"Look, Fran," Billy said, "Steven told us about your

little hitting problem. Well, that's okay, we have a lot of guys on the team who can hit pretty good. But I'm sure you can still throw and catch a ball, right?"

Number one, no one on the team could hit as well as I used to, and, number two, of course I could still catch and throw! But I choked those words back and just tried to go Zen again.

"You didn't even want me on the team a week ago," I said pleasantly.

"Oh, that." Billy waved his hand.

Oh, that? "I said, I quit."

Just like I knew he would, Billy lost it. "We're playing the Flyers tomorrow!" he screamed.

"Why does it matter to you?" I screamed back.

"HEY!" Steven yelled.

The river murmured and the trees sighed as Billy and I glared at each other.

"You owe us," Billy accused me.

"For what? For making my life hell?"

"Foster would have killed you—"

"Whooooaaa," Steven said. "Fran held her own against Foster. She got a piece of everything he threw at her."

Billy was still frowning, but I noticed Angel and Blast were looking at me with respect.

"But it took the whole team to bring that guy

down," Steven continued. "And it's going to take the whole team against the Foursquare Flyers tomorrow, too."

Yeah, right. "I'm just one player," I said. "You guys must have some friends who can play. I'm sure you can find a couple of stand-ins."

"Well . . . we can't," Steven said.

"We tried, but we're jinxed," Blast sputtered. "Nobody's parents will let them play for the Hardwares. They're afraid Foster will come back." He put his hands around his throat and made a strangling sound. "Like the creature who won't die in some horror movie."

Angel said, "The parks department is calling around, but even they can't find us a coach. Everyone's given up on us."

It seemed pretty clear to me that they should just forget the whole thing. Forfeit the game tomorrow. Enjoy the rest of the summer. I told them so. It was the new me talking, the one that didn't give two cents about baseball.

They stared at me like I was speaking Urdu.

"You know," Billy said, "I never liked you, but at least you weren't a quitter."

"Until now, I guess," Blast said.

Steven tried to explain their position one more

time. "We need you, Franny—we want to beat those guys. We're a team—it won't matter if you're in a slump. We can work around it. You can help out other ways."

I wished he wouldn't keep referring to The Flinch as a slump. A slump was bad, but you could get over it.

"Just one more game," Steven said.

But if I came back, if I played one more game, I'd have to give it up a second time. That would kill me.

"We're even trying to get word to Hootie," Billy said. "If we can sneak him out, I bet he'll come. I bet Hootie's not a quitter."

"Just tomorrow," Steven pleaded. "Just one more game. And then you can give it up, Fran. It doesn't matter if you can't hit. You're still our best fielder."

Suddenly my whole body felt hot. I scooped some water from the river and washed it over my face. Sunburn, maybe. Or maybe . . .

I wished that Aunt Beth hadn't taught me to look so carefully at things, because all of a sudden, when I looked up at Steven and Billy, Angel and Blast, for a flickering second I thought I saw Cullers' Classic All Stars.

This time, my imagination really had gone too far.

"I told you, I quit."

Pinc.

  Pinc.

    Pinc.

I pulled the covers off my head and stared up at my bedroom ceiling. The bare, tack-marked walls reflected a greenish light from the tree outside, and a long-legged wasp bumped against the window screen.

Pinc.

I picked up the count: fourteen, fifteen.

Pinc.

Then I woke up. Thrashing free of the sheets, I kneeled at the foot of the bed and stared down into the backyard. The pitcher was hidden by the angle of the house, but one by one, in an even rhythm, Ping-Pong balls were bouncing off the garage door. Steven, I deduced, back to harass me with another one of his Spawn of Slow pep talks.

I struggled into some jeans and started to run downstairs. Outside my door I hesitated, then I turned back and found a hairbrush. *Pinc. Pinc.* I could hear it even in the bathroom. Why did I care if Steven saw me all sleep-scraggled again—was I becoming MacKenzie? I threw down the brush and rushed down the stairs. There was a better view of the backyard from the window on the second-floor landing, so I stopped and jimmied the window open. When Steven saw the look on my face, he'd want to get a good running start—

It was Dad pitching.

The shock almost blew me back up the stairs. He stood with his back to the house, contemplating the garage door. He shifted his weight backwards, lifted his leg, traced an arc, threw.

Pinc.

He scratched his head, bent down, and picked three more balls out of the bag.

Pinc. Pinc. Pinc.

He nodded, stooped and picked up another ball, did it again. Did it again and again. Twenty-nine, I counted, thirty-two.

Thirty-three, but in slow motion this time. Taking it apart, concentrating on each movement . . . remembering how.

I held on to the windowsill as tight as I could; I felt more weightless than the wasp upstairs, like if I let go I might float away. For half an hour I watched as my dad worked his way steadily through the pile at his feet, as another and then another Ping-Pong ball sailed at the garage door, as he picked up speed and regained form.

Finally, he was done. He gathered the balls into the mesh bag, walked across the lawn, pushed it back under Aunt Beth's lawn chair, wiped his palms against his jeans, and set off down the driveway. Sort of jaunty.

After a long time, I felt the weight return to my body. I eased my grip on the windowsill, then tested the stairs: gravity still worked.

"Aunt Beth?" I looked for her in the kitchen, but she wasn't there. I padded across the cool linoleum and stared into the backyard. Outside, heavy white clouds moved across the sky, heaven moving from this place to that. Dad had missed a ball; the breeze dribbled it down the drive. The asphalt was rough under my bare feet as I chased the ball toward the street. Just before my fingers touched it, I stopped. I watched the ball roll along the curb and into a storm drain.

"Aunt Beth?" She wasn't on the front porch, or in her studio, either, but the light was blinking on the answering machine. Slow's voice crackled over the tape. "Franny? Hey there, champ—"

But I'm not—I'm no champ—so I hit rewind.

chapter 14

"I'm here for the massacre," I yelled.

Steven punched his fist at the sky.

"Get over it," I said as I stomped across the infield. "Nobody can save this team from the Flyers."

Mozzie and Blast popped out of the dugout. Were they really smiling at me?

"What made you change your mind?" Steven asked cheerfully.

"None of your business. Besides, it's just this one game."

"Unless we make the playoffs."

"Ha. Ha. Ha." Clearly Steven needed reminding.

I pointed toward the parking lot. "We won't make the playoffs."

Every kid from Tiny Tots to Junior League recognized the team van of the Foursquare Flyers. How could you miss it? Fluffy white wings were painted along the navy-blue sides, and gold letters spelled out "Sponsored by God."

The South Highwater Foursquare Baptist Church was so big they were trying to break away from South Highwater and start their own city; they were so rich they employed their own sports director, who had hired Tommy DeLucca, an ex–third baseman for the Marlins' AA farm team, to coach their Junior League team. Thanks to Mr. DeLucca, the Flyers wore professional-looking uniforms and threw professional plays. They acted professional, too: quiet, remote, polite. A real five-man video crew broadcast their games on a church cable channel.

The van doors slid open, and as the Flyers poured across the field, they swept past the Three Most Popular Girls in Junior High. MacKenzie clapped her hand over her heart and fell against Tiffany's shoulder. On top of everything, the Flyers were boy-band beautiful.

"Hey, guys," called a heavenly blond with wide shoulders. The sun practically glinted off his teeth as he smiled. It was like a cheesy TV commercial. "I hear you Hardwares are awesome. We're looking forward to a great game today!"

"Oh, retch." Billy sauntered out from behind the dugout.

The sparkle on the blond's smile flickered out, but the Flyers kept their cool. "Prayer circle, guys," said the blond, and then, to Billy, "We'll pray for you."

"No, we'll pray for *you!*" Billy snarled, but the Flyers ignored his lame comeback. They jogged over to their dugout and stood with their arms around one another's shoulders, hushed.

My turn. Billy looked over and did a fake double-take. "Girl germs," he sneered. Then he stuck his fist out at me. It took me a second to understand. . . . I reached out, too, and we bumped knuckles.

"Boy germs."

Billy nodded. "Cool."

Mr. DeLucca trailed his team across the infield. "Where's that coach of yours?" he called. "Prison?" He chuckled at his own joke, but he looked concerned. "You guys got someone else lined up?"

You could hear the chalk drifting from the baselines.

"Yeah," Steven said, finally. I raised my eyebrows at

him. He whispered, "The parks department dug up some old dude who hasn't coached in two or three years. Not sure who. I'm not even sure he'll make it."

Maybe I should have felt more cheerful. Wherever Coach Foster was, it probably involved armed guards. The Hardwares were staring defeat in the face. This situation was the answer to my dreams, but instead here I was, as low as the rest. In a few minutes I was going to walk up to the plate and introduce The Flinch to all my recent enemies. That would be good for some laughs. Quitting was the right solution, but since this morning a refrain had been running around and around my head. It was that dumb "Jackie played honorably until the final inning" speech. Slow still had me caught in the hot box between champ and anti-champ. I still cared.

This game *was* the final inning, I promised myself. Tomorrow morning I'd be retired. *Honorably* retired.

"When's that coach going to show up?" Blast said. He was wearing the do-rag again, and I noticed his legs were wrapped with bandages. He smelled smoky.

"Like we care?" Billy snorted. "This guy doesn't know us. He's never even seen us play. They're sending us a babysitter, that's all. We could ask anyone. We could ask . . . Chauppette's mom."

Billy stuck his tongue in his cheek and smirked.

"Hey, guys, let's ask Mrs. Chauppette to babysit." His singsongy voice suggested activities other than baseball. Steven just *launched* and called Billy a name I didn't think Steven even knew. I guess Billy has that effect on people. Even his so-called friends.

Billy and Steven went eyeball to eyeball, but before a fight could get started in earnest, Quoc piped up. "Maybe they'll send us a coach like DeLucca," he said hopefully.

Billy hooted (right up Steven's nostril). "Ex-pros don't exactly line up to coach Highwater Junior League, Quack."

"Oh yeah?" Steven growled (a quarter-inch from Billy's eye).

"Yeah!"

Great. I'd just made peace with Billy, and now I'd have to jump in and save Steven. Just in the nick of time, Steven stepped back, hands on hips; Billy smirked, but I could tell Steven wasn't giving in. He raised his right hand and pointed toward the parking lot. A creepy feeling prickled my scalp.

Steven's lips barely moved. "Well. There's one now."

It was just like the cartoons—everyone's head snapped around.

"That fat guy?" Billy jeered.

That fat guy had a head of blazing orange. I tried to

run, but my cleats were hammered into the dirt. The prickly feeling moved from my head down my neck into my armpits as I remembered the messages I'd been erasing.

Steven was jumping up and down like we were stranded in the wilderness and he was flagging a rescue plane.

"Slow! Slow!"

Slow McGonnagle lumbered across the field. Billy was going "hee-hee-hee" and "ho-ho-ho," but Steven ignored him and enthusiastically recited Slow's résumé to the rest of the team. With every step across the field, Slow's biography grew more impressive, until by the time he reached center field the Hardwares thought he'd managed the Yankees, as he ambled past second base he'd coached the Yanks to ten (twenty maybe) World Series, and by the time he reached the dugout Slow was so famous that if they'd had paper there'd have been confetti and a parade.

I was nailed to the dirt. *"Introduce me to your friend,"* *hissed The Flinch.*

"Why haven't you returned my calls?!" Slow boomed.

"I . . ."

"Your friends have to drive five hundred miles just

for a little chat?" He reached out and laid his hand around the back of my neck, and my legs nearly buckled under the weight. "Hello, HARDWARES!" His voice vibrated through me. "I hear you guys need a coach."

Everyone except Billy giggled. Steven beamed. Quoc even clapped—ex-pros did line up to coach Junior League!

"So I brought one along." Slow jerked his thumb over his shoulder. Parents were still streaming in from the parking lot; a car trunk slammed, and a man swung an equipment bag over his shoulder.

The only sound was the *thap, thap, thap*, of balls hitting Flyer mitts.

Slow slapped my back because I had stopped breathing.

"Who's that?" Mozzie asked, at the very same moment Billy made the rude sound you'd expect him to make. As he came closer, the man kept glancing back at the parking lot, like he wished he hadn't come.

Steven asked, "So, then, you're the assistant coach?"

"Nah. That man doesn't need an assistant coach," Slow said proudly. "That man has a keen eye for talent. He really knows how to motivate his players. He used to coach the Rosewood Baggers, you know!"

"Which league? American or National?" Quoc demanded.

Billy groaned. "You geek. The Rosewood Baggers are a Little League team over in Willamette. That's Fran's dad."

chapter 15

"Play ball!"

Mozzie pulled the catcher's mask over his face. Without a ninth player we almost had to forfeit, until Mr. DeLucca took pity and loaned us a fielder. Steven volunteered to fill Hootie's position, but his Tom Seaver fantasies were hammered out of him by the Flyer sluggers. *Blam! Thunk! Ker-POW!* It was just like the funny papers, except not funny.

I ran myself stupid, but at least it kept my mind off The Flinch. I charged in, I scooted right, I covered Blast, I sped back, chasing, chasing, chasing the Flyers' arsenal. I snagged a line drive and shot it to George, who just missed a tag at second. I chased a fly down and relayed it to Billy, who fired it home just as another runner slid in. Mozzie screamed and dropped the ball. "That hurts, man!"

Dad was useless. He just stood on the sidelines and watched the entire gory inning unfold. One hundred balls to remember how to pitch this morning? It might take him one hundred years to remember how to coach. He opened his mouth, he tugged on his hat brim, he shut his mouth. He shook his head, he shuffled his feet, he looked around helplessly. I kept my eye on the ball and tried not to watch. If I glanced at him by accident, or if I looked up at Slow when he screamed my name, then the world went all zigzaggy, and what good was that?

After seven runs, the Flyers staged a series of made-for-TV bloopers designed to move the game along and retired their side.

Bottom of the first. The Flyers' pitcher put Angel away one, two, three. Mozzie just watched the strikes whiz past his nose. Blast swung at everything, connected with nothing. I stood shoulder to shoulder along the fence with Steven as he called encouragement: "Focus," and "See the ball, hit the ball," and "Make them pitch to *you*," and useless advice like that. In the midst of this slaughter, it occurred to me, maybe no one would notice The Flinch.

"Advice?" Billy yelled at Dad.

Dad just shook his head and ignored the name Billy called him. I kept hoping he'd confer with Slow—a glance, a nod, sign language, telepathy, anything! But no, he just pressed a finger to his lips and watched Blast detonate as the last strike blew past him. We grabbed our mitts. Eight more innings of torture.

"Hold up, guys. Uh, I think I've seen enough," Dad said.

"Oh, goody for you, will you go home now?" Billy mocked. Two years ago, Dad would have yelled "Insubordination!" and benched the culprit, but not today. He put his hands on his hips, then in his pockets, then back on his hips, searching for the right position. I blamed Slow—obviously he'd dragged my dad here today, and where was he now? Over on the Flyers' side, swapping stories with Mr. DeLucca. I couldn't take it. I just looked away and concentrated on tomorrow morning, when I'd be retired and could go back to painting flowers.

"Let me tell you one strategy of a winning team," Dad said quietly. (A bitter laugh: Billy.) "They try to bury you early." He looked around expectantly. No one had a clue what he was talking about. He scratched his head nervously. "So . . . the Flyers screwed up. I think."

Billy said, "The first inning? Seven runs? We're not buried?"

Our borrowed fielder blushed and slunk away from our conference.

Dad pressed his lips together. Then the words came out in a rush, like he was making it up on the fly. "They could have had a lot more. Didn't you notice those errors were intentional? The Flyers don't want to be here all night, and, besides, let me tell you one thing about the Flyers. Nice boys."

Dad looked at us like we were supposed to do something with that information. "Nice. Mmm-hm." He nodded, then snickered. "Bless them." He laughed alone.

The ump cleared his throat impatiently.

Dad sighed. "Steven, I'm sorry. As I remember, you were a great first baseman, and I need a long, tall lefty in that position right now." He took the ball from Steven, who didn't look too disappointed. Then he handed it to Billy. "You, I think, are *not* a nice boy."

Billy started to sneer, but his lip got stuck halfway up his face. He just stared at what he held in his hands.

"Those balls you were throwing from third? Like that. Just keep it legal."

I wished the Flyers' video crew could catch the stunned look on Billy's face. I'd buy a copy of the tape.

"Okay, you"—Dad pointed at Blast—"how bad are those injuries?"

"I'll live," Blast threatened.

"Well, today you're on death's door," Dad said. Suddenly he smiled. It wasn't his weak actor's smile, either. "You're catcher. Every time a Flyer comes home, I want you to stand in front of the plate and scream and moan and wave your bandages in the air."

Blast pulled the do-rag off his head. Dad looked at his crusty scalp and grinned, a full-blown "This might not hurt so bad after all" grin.

"Beautiful! Flash that around a little. I guarantee you those Flyers are too nice to hurt you. Just *block that plate*."

"Let's play ball!" the ump shouted.

Dad was talking in a rush now. "Franny, you're third, but you've also got to cover short. Who's this?" Hootie had tiptoed up behind us. The team cheered, Quoc threw his arms around Hootie, the Flyer ran back to his team, and Dad looked relieved when he realized he now had a full set of Hardwares.

Third base! I galloped out to the infield, the sun heating my shoulders, the wind cooling my cheeks, *that oily Flinch tightening its bony arms around my neck, drawing me into its sticky chest, its tarry lips muttering in my ear*—I stopped running. I couldn't breathe.

While Dad sorted out the other positions, Mozzie helped Blast into the catcher's gear. Billy walked out to the mound, stepped up and toed the rubber, and stared, stock-still, at the batter. The wind picked up the edges of his blond hair. Blast crouched behind home, the oversized chest pad propping him up. He gave an experimental moan.

Suddenly Blast popped up and smiled. He turned his mitt over and stared at it.

"Strike?" the umpire asked.

"Yes!" Steven screamed from first. "Yeesss!"

Okay, I'm exaggerating. The pitch wasn't *quite* that fast. Hands on my knees, I was gasping for air, but at the last moment I lifted my head and I saw Billy throw the ball. The same way you see a bolt of lightning—it's there and then it's gone.

God switched sides—it's the only explanation.

"Steee-rike two!"

"Yeee-haaaaa!" Billy arched his chest, threw his arms wide, and screamed at the sun. "YAAAAAA!!!"

It was the same fastball he'd been shooting around the diamond all season, but with a proper windup, and a little time to aim, it was fast enough that the Flyers' hitter was still looking for it ten seconds after it had crossed the plate.

"Strike three!" The Flyers' boy looked like he'd been mugged.

"Go, Billy!" screamed the Three Most Popular Girls, who until this very moment had been exchanging phone numbers with the enemy. Now they scurried back over to the Hardwares' bleachers. The rest of the Hardware fans sat bug-eyed and slack-jawed.

"Good call, J.J.!" Slow yelled.

"Time out!" Mr. DeLucca asked to inspect the ball. The ump handed it to him, and a herd of Flyers dads deserted the stands and clustered around the coach as he inspected the ball for a foreign substance. Spit. Gum. Magic whatever. Slow pushed his way through the throng, slapped Mr. DeLucca on the shoulder, and bent to inspect the ball, too. There was a faint smile on his lips as he watched Mr. DeLucca squinting. Finally, the coach shook his head and handed the ball back to the ump. Clean.

But the second slugger strutted onto the field with confidence. Sure, one hitter was down. But they were still the Foursquare Flyers. I held my breath. Would Billy choke? Perhaps we had all been hallucinating.

"Strike one." Mr. DeLucca pulled a cell phone out of his navy-blue jacket. "Strike two!" He punched speed dial, paced back and forth, anxious for someone in a distant town to answer. "Steeee-rike three!" With barely a nod to his defeated hitter, Mr. DeLucca pushed the next boy out and started jabbering into his phone. I imagined a big-time scout pulling a suitcase out of his closet and racing to catch the next flight to Portland. The future I had once dreamed for myself would be Billy's.

He'd been practicing. Why, I wondered, hadn't he asked to pitch before? Coach Foster always put Hootie on the mound, of course, but when the game started today and Dad asked who wanted to pitch, Steven stuck his hand up, not Billy.

Billy had been afraid of looking stupid.

I liked him a little better.

For about .00002 of a second.

"Ha-ha!" Billy yelled as the third Flyer struck out. Like the class act he is, he rolled his tongue in his cheek, stuck out his butt, and spanked himself. Blast lit an imaginary stick of dynamite and threw it after the defeated player.

"Okay, okay." Dad waved the team in around him. The Hardwares were leaping like lottery winners, and Billy clutched my father as if Dad had passed him the winning ticket. Only I stood back.

The Flinch oozed up my shadow and ran a cold finger along my spine.

It said: I'm still here.

"So what?" Dad growled. "They still have seven runs. What do we have?" He made a circle with his thumb and forefinger and stared at us through the hole in the middle. "Now, I think Billy can hold these guys off, and our friend Slow over there has gathered some interesting notes on their pitcher. . . ."

Dad nodded to Slow, who still loitered over by the Flyers' dugout. Slow looked around to make sure he wasn't being watched, then held up one finger. "That means a fastball," Dad said.

Slow flashed two fingers. "Curve." Three fingers. "Change up." Four fingers. "Slider."

"Aren't we cheating?" asked the only kid on the team who'd care (Steven).

Dad didn't even hesitate. "Nope. The catcher has a responsibility to hide his signs. That kid's practically painting them on a billboard. Who's up?"

The first pitch went whizzing by him, but George watched Slow carefully, then stepped into a curveball and doubled.

"Yeah!" Slow gave Dad a thumbs-up.

I counted down until it was my turn. *The Flinch counted, too.*

George's success was inspirational. Billy smacked a line drive between short and third for a single.

Hardware fans, moms and dads who usually packed it up and trailed away mid-game, now screamed and hollered and pounded the boards with their feet, and then one man stood up and threw an empty soda can at the Flyers' stands. It only soared a few feet before it clattered to the alley between the bleachers . . . but still.

Steven sat down beside me on the bench. "You okay?" he whispered. "It probably won't happen again, Fran." He nudged me with his elbow. He wanted me to smile, but I couldn't.

Quoc was up. Me next. Everyone was hitting off the Flyers' pitcher now. Everyone would notice when I couldn't.

"Franny! You're on deck." Far away, Dad called.

The Flinch said: Shall we go now?

My knees were locked, but somehow I staggered out of the dugout. From the corner of my eye I saw Dad approach. "Franny . . . why didn't you tell me?"

I could barely hear him over the slithery voice in my head. *C'mon, c'mon! The Flinch hissed.*

"About Coach Foster, I mean. To have to hear from Mrs. Chauppette . . ."

Quoc sent the ball soaring right past short. George and Billy scrambled around the bases as the fans cheered.

Today was nice, but tomorrow, after Dad had seen The Flinch, after I had to give up baseball a second time . . . tomorrow I'd have to learn to live without him again, too.

"I'm quitting," I mumbled.

"Huh?" Dad bent his knees and stared at my face. "Did you just say you're quitting? But you're on deck."

"After today. I'm quitting baseball. Forever."

The way he laughed, it's like I was the San Diego Famous Chicken. "*You?* Quitting baseball?" He chuckled up at the sky. When he finally stopped, he said, "What a beautiful day—I forgot grass smells this good. Okay, slugger, you're up."

The Flinch dragged me to the plate, it stepped behind me, its claws digging into my shoulders, ready to yank me back.

It said: Your dad is back, but you, Fran, are gone, gone, gone.

c h a p t e r   1 6

"So, do you have a name for that?" Slow ran across the infield and snatched the bat away from me. He pulled a dollar bill out of his back pocket and started rubbing it along the wood—old pro voodoo.

"The Flinch."

"Good name," Slow said. He rubbed so hard he looked like he was trying to start a fire. "Fine name. PERFECT name."

Mozzie grounded into a double play to end the inning. The Flyers streamed past me, and the Hardwares ran onto the field. Steven touched my arm as he jogged by, but no one else would look at me.

Dad stood with his palm pressed to his forehead. He couldn't look, either.

"I'll work on this," Slow promised, rubbing so hard the dollar bill nearly ripped in half.

I crouched beside third base, but it was like I was underwater—my eyes kept pooling. I pulled my brim lower over my face so no one could see. Be tough, be tough, I told myself. But I was tired of being tough— I'd used my last bit of tough to get me to the game today, and now I was empty. Hunching lower, I stared at the watery dirt.

The game swirled on around me. Would it ever end? The Flyers wondered, too. Then, in the fourth inning, the Flyers' prayers were answered. Billy's hot-dogging wrecked his aim, and he loaded the bases on walks. He didn't panic, though; he quieted down and regained control. But the next boy clocked Billy's fastball and slammed it deep into right field. Finally, Blast had his moment. He staggered down the third baseline screaming "Medic!" and the confused Flyer running in from third stopped to render aid while his teammates piled up behind him, eager to help. Billy tagged all *four* out. That didn't happen again. Mr. DeLucca called his team names they'd never learned in Sunday school, and from that point on, even if Blast had set himself on fire, he couldn't have begged a Tylenol off that squad.

Shortly after, Mr. DeLucca realized we'd stolen their signs and chased Slow away, but confidence worked wonders on my teammates' batting ability. The Hardwares had taken a long look and noticed an interesting detail about the Flyers: they were thirteen years old. Just like us. The Hardwares fed off that.

I Flinched.

The Flyers got some more hits off Billy, so Dad pulled him aside and showed him a four-seam fastball that put more movement on his rocket. That helped.

I Flinched.

Slow did everything he could think of. He drew a circle in the dirt around my bat and chanted an old Indian charm over it. Dad said he was calling in special help and went to use Mrs. Chauppette's cell phone, but even if he was calling in the Devil to make a deal, it was too late. The heavenly blond walked over and offered to pray, and Slow said sure, the more the merrier.

I Flinched.

The score narrowed: Flyers 9, Hardwares 5. Flyers 10, Hardwares 7. Fighting for every run, we were gaining on them. Flyers 13, Hardwares 11.

The Flyers stayed cool, but their parents freaked.

One dad walked out along the third-base path. "Jimmy," he called to his son, who was facing Billy. He reached for his wallet and pulled out a bill, then held it high over his head. I'd heard of this tradition, fans offering dollars for home runs. Jimmy blanched. His father was holding up a twenty.

"Strike three." By now there were five fathers on the third-base path holding up twenties for the next boy. Fishing through her purse, a woman joined them. She had a fifty.

The Three Most Popular Girls in Junior High thought up a special cheer called "Billy Ball," and the Hardwares' bleachers swayed as everyone sang along. A Flyers fan threw a soda can back at the Hardware stands; it hit the boards and sprayed Dr Pepper all over. Mrs. Chauppette screamed. Aunt Beth drove up and came running across the field holding a paper bag, then stopped and watched wide-eyed as men poured from the benches and ran at each other. Somebody's father threw a punch. Whistles blew. The umps and a few of the cooler-headed adults were pulling people apart. One guy had a bloody nose, and a woman limped away across the field.

The Flyers widened their lead, but we remained optimistic.

"Patience. One run at a time," Dad coached. Steven

hit a nice line drive to left field for a double, then stole third. Angel drove him in. Mozzie was thrown out at first, Blast singled, and George doubled him in. I Flinched.

Slow cornered me in the dugout. "Let me tell you what Johnny Bench said about hitting slumps. 'They're like bed. Easy to get into and hard to get out of.' Now let me tell you what Yogi Berra said—" I escaped.

Next inning, Steven doubled, and Angel brought him in. "Fight for it!" Dad yelled, pacing the sidelines. I Flinched. He motioned for me, but I went and stood behind the bleachers, stared at the grass. I wiped my cheek. Could it get any worse?

Yes. Much, much worse. I knew how. I saw it coming. Just like in my morning games on the back lawn, when I was the only one who could save the game— that's how bad it could get.

And that's how bad it *did* get.

Bottom of the ninth. Two outs against the Hardwares. Quoc on first, Billy on second, and George on third. *Crack!* A man on the bottom plank of the Flyers' stands uncorked a bottle of champagne, and someone else was passing out plastic cups with little screw-on stems. The Flyers were still three runs ahead and it was time to celebrate. The girl was up next. She was no challenge at all.

"Franny!" Far away, over the roar of the crowd, Aunt Beth called.

"I'm almost done," I mumbled.

Steven was standing in my way. He grabbed my arm. "You're tough," he said. I pushed past him.

Time to get this over with.

The Flinch wants the girl.

Sweat lathered my palms as I cocked the bat over my shoulder. There were so many pitches in the world, and I couldn't hit any of them. The pitcher tape-measured me in a glance. He reared back . . . NO! I couldn't do it.

I Flinched.

The crowd erupted. On third base, George passed a hand over his eyes. Someone turned on a boom box, and the Flyers boogied to Christian rap while the cable crew zoomed in on the boys' jubilant faces. One lone camera was trained on me.

"OVERCOME!" Steven bellowed.

"Strike two!"

"Heh-heh," said The Flinch.

"Fran!" Billy yelled. "You didn't even swing!" The pitcher heard that, and a big "Gotcha now" smirk spread across his face. She didn't even swing! One more pitch and the girl's history.

"Time out!" Dad called.

I caught the ump's sleeve. "No, let me get it over with."

"Your coach is calling you. Time out."

I turned and watched Dad come scuffling across the diamond. He carried the brown bag Aunt Beth had brought with her. He pulled me out of the batter's box.

"Honey, this is one hell of a slump you're in. I've never seen anything like it. Even Slow . . . Well, he doesn't have any suggestions."

I looked over his shoulder. Slow drooped in the dugout beside Blast, digging in the dirt with his toes. He looked like he might cry.

I tried to say something, but my lips felt stitched together. I concentrated on the sweat stains spreading across Dad's shirt. He sighed. "There's only one last thing we can try." He unrolled the top of the bag, reached in, and pulled out a ball. I didn't recognize it at first. Then I saw the signature and the dust bunny clinging to it. "Here. Touch it."

I didn't believe in it anymore. It was only a cold leather ball. But to make him happy, I reached for it anyway.

150

He pulled it back. "Oh no. You don't get to hold it. Just touch it."

I looked up to see if he was kidding. He wasn't.

"You've had it for over a year, right?" he said. "So I get it for a year, too."

"Dad. That's not fair."

"Then we're back to the weekly schedule."

"Dad!"

The ump cleared his throat and reminded us that there was a game after this one and the guys wanted to warm up.

"Quick, take off your helmet." Dad rolled the McGwire Ball over my scalp. "Don't worry about The Flinch," he whispered. "I know it feels awful. But we'll work on it together, okay? Me, you, Crabby, and Mac."

"Suck it up and lose already!" someone yelled.

The ump cleared his throat, so I turned and stumbled back to the plate.

"You mean Camp Carmichael? The Big Trip?" I had to yell to be heard over the Flyers' boom box.

"Week of August 18. The session was sold out, but Slow pulled some strings."

Before I stepped up to the plate, I pretended to toy with my glove. When did Dad start using his real voice again? When he rolled the McGwire Ball over my head? The ball was magic, after all, because when it touched me it told me something: all these months, when Dad was using that strange voice, when I was practicing living without him, he was practicing something, too. He was practicing being a dad again.

Now he had it down solid.

The pitcher nodded, but there was no respect in his eyes. I settled over the plate. I'd thrown away two pitches and now I only had one chance. I didn't think I could do it. I didn't think I was tough enough.

I gulped. . . . He reared back. . . .

No one saw what happened next.

The ball came whizzing at me. The Flinch grabbed my shirt and started to pull, but I reached behind me and caught its sticky wrist, yanked it over my shoulder, slammed it against the plate, stabbed it with my cleats, snatched the ball right out of the air, picked The Flinch up by its scrawny little neck, and wrapped it like chewing gum around and around the ball. Then I heaved it up with all my strength and hammered that thing into the thin blue sky.

You can't take this away from me.

Everyone else just saw me hit an amazing fly to deep center field.

"Run!" Steven yelped.

"GOGOGOGOGOGOGO!" Slow was screaming.

I just stood there and watched the ball carrying

The Flinch higher and higher. It couldn't breathe up there. It died.

"RUN!" screamed the Hardwares. Aunt Beth had her arms around Mrs. Chauppette. They were jumping up and down in the bleachers. "RUUUUUNNN!" thundered the spectators.

Good advice. I raced for first. The center fielder was chasing after the ball, but he couldn't reach it. It bounced to the wall, he ran it down, snagged it as I scrambled past second. But I wasn't worried—I was flying! It didn't matter if they tagged me out, it didn't matter if we lost this game, it wasn't the last, there were innings and innings still to play. I had to tell Dad something—now—and if it weren't for the roar of the crowd, I'd yell it to him as I ran: I could grow old without seeing Cooperstown, I didn't care about Camp Carmichael, I didn't want to meet McGwire, and I didn't give a hoot about the Yankees anymore. *This* was what I wanted—this lumpy field, this crooked diamond, this league, this team, this day, this coach.

Sorrow might hit you like a hundred-mile-an-hour beanball, but happiness can surprise you, too.

"Stay on third!" Steven screamed, but I flew around it. Quoc, Billy, and George had scored, and the Hardwares were dancing behind home plate. Slow was hopping along the baseline—"No! Go back! Oh! Oh! C'MON! MOVE IT!"

The second baseman made the relay throw. I knew the ball was blazing down upon me. I put my head down and charged for home.

Dad knew I'd make it. He crossed his arms and grinned.

The catcher reached for the ball—*thap!* He had it—he crouched—

I punched my leg out, I was airborne, I hit the dirt sliding. . . .

The ump cried, "Safe!"